THREE DAYS IN DECEMBER

A Novel

SLADE AUSTIN

Three Days in December

© Copyright 2016 Slade Austin

All rights reserved.

BookWise Publishing, Riverton, Utah
bookwisepublishing.com

ISBN:978-1-60645-169-4 Paperback
ISBN: 978-1-60645-170-0 Ebook

Library of Congress:: 2016956263

First Printing

To Liz
May you continue the example
of grace and strength that
the remarkable women
in your family possessed.

Acknowledgments

I would like to acknowledge my mother for her fortitude and her grace; my brothers for the influence they had on my life; Cindee for being such a supportive parent to Liz; Rick and Keri Evans for their steadfast encouragement; my grandparents for their strength; Rebecca for her vision; Karen for her prodding (in a good way); MG for showing me love; Cody for such swagger; Jason Wells for being a true friend; and Woody because he is a truly a good human.

—Slade Austin

Chapter 1

My grandfather's words still rung in my mind as I wandered the picked through Christmas stock at Rite-Aid. I was surprised at the number of people still out shopping for cheap candy canes, pretzels covered in third-rate chocolate, small ceramic Santas, and China-born welcome signs with plastic holly.

You would think an event planner would be on top of every detail for his own Christmas Eve party, but it doesn't happen that way. I didn't berate myself about this anymore; I had to learn to accept it. The cobbler's children are always barefoot, Grandpa would say. Everyone else's party is a priority and, for my party, well, it's at the end of the Christmas to-do list. Before going home to help Mom with details for tomorrow's event, I had to stop to buy guest favors for stocking stuffers. Rite-Aid was still open when I drove by after 9:00 o'clock, so I pulled in the parking lot. Surely they'd have fun stuff to put in the Christmas socks.

Next to me was a mother arguing with her young daughter. "We can't get those, Chloe. There's only five left and we need six." The daughter sighed heavily, "If we'd come yesterday we could have gotten them."

I walked to the end of the aisle to escape their bickering, only to be confronted with a young mother and a crying infant. When I looked down there were miniature tins of Russell Stover religious mints Mom, Gran and I called Jesus mints. At least the small blonde girl with holly in her hair on each box looked familiar and nostalgic. I picked up a couple dozen discounted boxes and put them in the cart. Discounted prices were the only reason to wait until tonight. The shopworn merchandise was tattered and sloppy, and I told myself never to wait this long again. The voices of the mother and daughter still carried down the aisle, and the glaring light of the drugstore washed out whatever loveliness there may have been in the colorful foil wrapping of the displayed candy. A man pushed past me and another woman bumped me with her shopping cart.

I was getting angry. Where was Christmas? Where was my daughter? We had always had so much fun buying the stocking stuffers for Christmas Eve. I backed my cart out of the aisle and wheeled it to the only quiet place in the store—cleansers and detergents. I pulled out my phone and called my daughter, Liz. She was in Kansas City with her mother, my ex-wife, Ann. Liz picked it up on the second ring.

"Hi, honey, it's Dad."

"Oh. Hi, Dad."

"I'm shopping for tomorrow night's party."

"Oh."

"I miss you, Liz. I wish you were here to help me with it."

"Oh, Daddy, I don't like shopping for candy and stuff like that anymore."

I felt my throat tighten. "I know, honey. You're growing up. But, I miss you."

"I miss you, too, Dad. Call me on Christmas, okay?"

"Yes, Liz, I'll call." My neck felt stiff. "I sent your present. You should have it."

"It came today. Gotta go. Bye, Dad."

"Bye, Liz."

I just stood there. Burl Ives' Have a Holly, Jolly Christmas played through the store, and at the end of the aisle, people rushed around frantically. I walked to the far end of the store, my fists balled in frustration.

A display of cellophane-wrapped perfumes caught my eye in particular—*White Shoulders* by Evyan. Its soft, pink box with the gold embossed cameo was a gentle, beckoning oasis in the middle of madness. The store sounds fell away, and my grandfather Pap's aging voice rang through me.

Let me tell you about my wife. It had been Christmas Eve over twenty years ago that I first heard those words. We were in a department store and Pap was leaning against me, his body in pain from the surgery he had undergone a few days earlier. His other long, strong arm was outstretched to a tired-looking clerk. "Let me tell you about my wife," he said.

"Do you see anything you like?" The tall woman forced herself to be polite through pursed lips.

That day so long ago had changed my life. I had to remember that. This is why I'm in this hapless store the night before Christmas Eve, I thought. Cheap stocking stuffers weren't the only reason I was here. I needed to buy *White Shoulders* for Gran.

When I got home I carefully opened the back door wide enough for Shadow's black nose to emerge. I stroked the black, mixed-breed German shepherd to calm him before I entered.

"Shhh, Jake, try not to make too much noise. Gran's asleep," Mom was at the kitchen table bent over spools of red grosgrain ribbon, wire, and her scissors.

"You're making more bows?" I asked

"Mother didn't think there were enough on the tree. She told me where they needed to be added, so here I am." Her dark, thick curls with only a few strands of silver loosely framed her face.

"You're a good bow maker."

"I've been at it a long time."

"Remember when you and great-grandma Pauline made about a hundred?"

She nodded, "Those were silver. That year Mother

wanted silver. 'Like snow sparkling under a winter's sunny sky,' she said."

"Want to see this sorry collection of things for the socks tomorrow night?" I waved the shopping bag. She laughed at the mints and assured me that the candy, Santa pens, and the holiday bottle openers would be fine.

"An orange at the bottom of the sock and Christmas cheer will dress everything right up." I didn't show her the White Shoulders.

I sat down to help her and we caught up on our days. She told me Gran had been bored with television, so she had invited our twelve-year-old neighbor to come play checkers. I told her that Ann had called to harangue me about a box she wanted me to send her. She'd carelessly left a pile of boxes in the garage and a few more in the basement, but she expected me to take the time to look for one she cared about. Mom sighed and nodded her head, but said nothing.

After half an hour she put the scissors down. "I'm going to bed. The rest can wait until morning."

"Good night."

I went to the living room to admire the tree. The brilliant white lights glowed, and broad gold ribbon was draped in precision down the ten foot tree. Every branch held an arranged collection of a gold or silver, filigreed butterfly, ornaments from every decade back to 1900, and a ceramic angel playing an instrument. But, of course, there were not enough red bows.

I should have been tired, and my body did feel worn from a long day, but my mind was racing with all I'd done and still needed to do before Christmas Eve. I sat on the couch with Shadow at my feet and let the magic of the tree calm me.

On the silk tree skirt were a dozen hand-carved wooden cars with rolling wheels Pap had made thirty years earlier. Their arrangement, placed with the precision of a department store window, showed as much skill as love for the man we still missed. Hanging on the wall next to the tree was an oil painting of Gran taken from a photo when she was in her thirties. Her fire for life and love for Pap shone through the paints as it still did from the clear eyes of the woman now sleeping down the hall.

People tell me that homemade wooden toys, cuff links, or a scratched, old wooden dining room table are only things. I'm told to sell them or give them away and move on. My friend Eric wasn't the first to tell me it's necessary to break ties with the past and become a new, evolved person. I knew he had meant well the night before as we talked about my failed marriage over dinner at the Oyster Bar. "Jake, I know this divorce has been hard on you, but you have to look forward to the future," he'd said.

"You mean after my grandmother dies," I said. He squirmed and I was sorry I'd been short with him, but everybody had been telling me I had taken on too much by inviting my grandmother and mother to live with me.

"The house felt so empty," I said.

"And you love your grandmother. I know your mother takes care of you both, but it's a lot of responsibility."

"No more than I had when I was married," I said. I changed the subject. "Ann called again to ask me to look for that stupid box." Eric straightened his slim frame before looking me in the eye. Whenever he did that I felt shorter than my five feet nine inches.

"Enough of her," he said, "It's time you become the real you and find a new partner without her as dead weight." He'd told me before to get rid of old stuff, quit thinking about my ex-wife, to move on, and leave my problems behind. I'd heard it all a dozen times.

As we parted ways in the parking lot, I reminded him of the party, "You're coming for Christmas Eve aren't you? Ham, turkey, everything will be there."

"And Ms. Alwida, too. She's the best part." Everyone liked visiting with Gran. "Of course. Carly and I will be there."

There was still a lot to do for the party, but reflecting in front of the tree had calmed my mind. All I could hear was Shadow's breathing. I got the *White Shoulders* I'd left in my coat pocket, and slipped the pink-papered, cellophane-wrapped box deep into the tree branches.

"C'mon boy, let's go to bed." I turned out the lights. Shadow headed for his nightly vigil at the foot of Gran's bed, and I headed to my room. On my way out of the room I passed my grandparents' old, round, dining room table and, as I looked at it, I realized that Eric just couldn't see the whole picture. He didn't know me when I was seventeen, or when the story really began when I was nine.

Above the table is a three foot piece of driftwood from Oregon that Gran burnished with an elk horn. Right in front of it are two round, gold cuff links that belonged to my grandfather, Matthew. Pap is what I came to call him, but not when I first met him as a nine-year-old.

If I moved on without these mementos and memories, I would be going into a future where I'd left an essential part of myself behind, a place where final good-byes had been said, and I wasn't supposed to think about them, or remember the people who had meant the most to me.

So, I am happy to be in this house where I know the quiet means my mother and grandmother are peacefully sleeping. It's often late at night when I feel their peace, and I can do my best work without interruption.

My company, Great Party! specializes in small and mid-size catering events. The company is growing and the bids require more time and creative presentation. Being in business for myself is both a blessing and a curse. That night I was planning on making progress on three proposals for events scheduled to be held in May, but tomorrow would have to do.

The next morning Gran and Mom were in the kitchen when I walked in. Gran, who had slowly become shorter than most twelve year-olds, was at the table waiting while Mom made toast and dished up peaches out of a mason jar harvested last summer from the peach tree in the back yard. Pushed to the end of the table were the ribbon, scissors, and wire for bows.

"I heard Annieconda called you yesterday."

"Yes, Gran, and her name is Ann."

"She's a snake to me. What did she want?"

"She wants me to go through the boxes again. I told her I already did."

"I have just one question. Who will she have to bitch at in Kansas City?"

It made me smile when she talked this way. Gran had always been such a fighter. But I didn't answer her because I didn't want her to get upset. She was too fragile, her health declining rapidly, and a head of steam wouldn't be good for her. Still, I liked that she was always ready to fight for me. Even now when I'm the strong one. I wish I could fight death for her. In her early thirties Gran had leukemia, but after treatment it had not returned until a year ago. "Disease wasn't allowed to live in me. I had too much to live for," she'd say as her chin pushed out.

"Here, Jacob, eat this." Mom handed me a plate with eggs and sausage. Only Mom or Gran ever used my given name Jacob, and when they did I knew was an order, so I ate a few bites before going.

Mom held her fork in the air as I headed out the door, "I've got most of it ready for tonight, but I sure would like your help earlier if you can get here."

"I'll try."

Whenever I walk through the doors of my company I feel proud. Besides Liz, it's the one good thing that came out of my marriage. Ironically, it is also what ruined it. Ann and I had started Great Party! five years earlier with just the two of us putting in sweat equity day and night. She ran the back by getting things physically organized with plates of finger food, table arrangements, and linens. She also rounded up our motley, part-time crew and turned them into a reasonable wait staff in starched shirts with combed hair and clean fingernails. I worked in the front office frantically calling food distributors, late employees, and ice companies until Ann appeared in the doorway to glare at me. That was her signal to hang up the phone and drive us to the event to set up. Bridesmaid parties, anniversaries, house weddings, dog birthdays for that matter; we took any job we could get in the beginning.

What started as a dream to be independent ended up tearing us apart. The marriage didn't survive, but the company has. The pressures of starting a new business, who was in charge of what, arguing over money that just wasn't there, and with no one else to talk to because we were together twenty-four hours a day starts the list of what went wrong. I don't blame her, but I also don't hold myself responsible for any more than fifty-percent of the problems. Even so, it's going to take a few years before both of us lose our residual anger and hurt.

I've learned my lesson, though. I hired a full-time event manager, Tim O'Donough, and a few months later Chef Don Sanchez. That morning they were both on-site when I walked in the door and headed to the office. It would be a slow day for me. People weren't calling about new events on Christmas Eve, so I could concentrate on a big bid scheduled for May.

The two small house parties Great Party! had for the day were meant to allow overstretched hosts to enjoy their own parties and were enough to keep a lean staff busy. As a thank you to our employees, Chef Don had made extra salads and desserts to split between us and the kids who came in to help him.

School was out for the holidays, so it was easier for Tim to rally enough teenagers and college students for a few hours of work. When I went back at two o'clock to talk to Tim, the kids had already started to roll in. We needed our small army of part-time helpers and bartenders.

Chef Don and I were discussing the assembly of an olive roll when I saw a kid who had been on maybe half a dozen jobs with us. He was a brown-haired, lanky boy who looked like he was having trouble holding up the long bones that were still growing. In a crowded high school hall no one would notice him, but seeing him alone, I registered his eyes for the first time. They were watchful and bordering on angry under dark, expressive eyebrows.

I nodded at him as he came closer, carrying several dozen plates to pack. His head barely moved to acknowledge me, which I'd come to expect with some of the kids. As he walked by I smelled the sweet, deep breath of cherry sloe gin. The smell immediately reminded me of my teenage years of being an alcoholic.

I interrupted Chef Don, "That boy, what's his name?"

"Logan."

"Has he been a good employee? How does he work?"

"Does his work. Never been a problem. Quiet."

I walked over to the group of kids packing flatware and napkins and caught Logan's eye. I signaled him over.

"You're Logan, right?"

"Yes." He stood about four feet away and turned his head.

Now I smelled breath mint. "Have you been drinking?"

"No."

I looked into his eyes. "Good. Because if you had, I'd have to let you go." I would have just sent him home for the day, but decided to scare him with what I could.

Logan just folded his arms and gave a slight nod so I walked away.

It was late afternoon when everyone was finally out of there and I could close up. I walked to the back loading area to make sure the garage door was locked, then I stopped by the kitchen to check on the stove, oven, and temperature of the freezer. Last, I stood by the front door, turned around to the darkness that now filled Great Party! and said, "Thank you. Thank you that I have gotten this far in life from where I started." Logan's face came to mind as I locked the door and headed to the car. There was still a lot to do tonight.

At six o'clock Mom, Gran, and I turned on the Christmas music of Frank Sinatra, Dean Martin, and Tony Bennett. I helped Gran from her walker to the couch where she could watch the crowd go by and hail any of them to come talk to her. She looked so frail in her light blue cashmere sweater. Only the light in her eyes and the line of her mouth still looked like the oil painting on the wall. Mom sat at the other end of the couch to gain her composure before people started arriving. I sat on the chair closer to the door. We all admired how the extra bows had made a difference on the Christmas tree.

"You did very well, Mary," Gran said.

"Thanks, Mother."

"With a little help and direction, of course."

"Yes."

"Looks great, Mom. It reminds me of the tree we had when I spent Christmas with Gran and Pap," I said.

"This tree isn't as pretty as that tree, Jake. That tree was perfect."

Guests started arriving and we were happy to see them. We hadn't always lived in Salt Lake City, but the friends we had collected over the last ten years meant the world to us. Eric and his long-time girlfriend, Carly, were the first to arrive, and they helped greet others while I started pouring drinks and encouraging people to eat.

Around nine o'clock I saw that all the excitement was starting to wear on Gran. She had been holding court for almost three hours, and though she loved to do it and came naturally by it, her frailty was showing. But she couldn't wear out yet; it was our tradition to open presents on Christmas Eve.

To encourage people to call it an evening, I brought out the huge basket of stuffed Christmas socks meant to be good-bye favors. Mom was right, they did look better under the lights of Christmas party cheer. A few people did leave, and then a few more when I offered to wrap leftover desserts to take home.

I love my friends. I love Christmas Eve, but there was an urgency to spend extra time this Christmas Eve with only Gran and Mom visiting and opening presents. What I didn't want to think about was that it could be Gran's last. The three of us needed to be together in front of our beautiful tree. Finally, the last guests left. Before we even heard the start of their car, Mom, Gran, and I were gathered in front of the tree. Susan Boyle's transporting voice was singing Hallelujah.

"It was a good party," Gran said.

Mom and I nodded.

"Let's listen to Frank Sinatra."

I got up and changed the music. The iconic voices of the forties and fifties were as much a part of my childhood as hand-carved wooden toys and burnished Oregon driftwood. Music always played at Pap and Gran's. Dean Martin came on singing Silver Bells.

In silence we listened to most of the song. "Dean's voice always takes me back to when I met my Matt." We were quiet until Gran spoke again. "He was such a handsome man."

"Which one, Dean or Pap, Gran? They were both there," I smiled.

"Matt. Matt. But Dean was handsome, too. His voice is what I noticed. Across a dance floor with a hundred people he was singing only to you. At least that's what every woman in the room wanted him to do."

"That was a job with benefits."

"I enjoyed my work."

"And you were good at it. Numbers and columns of figures were meant for you."

"I grew up around moon-shining. You have to be fast with numbers when those old thieves showed up. Besides, it was the best way to make a living in Steubenville, Ohio.

"Especially for a single mom," my mom said.

"You deserved a better start, Mary."

"It was fine, Mother. I was with family."

"That you were. Aunts, uncles, cousins everywhere. The same group of troublemakers I grew up with." Tree lights were lighting Gran's face with a glow I hadn't seen for a long time. It added life that I wanted always to be there. "Being manager of that nightclub finally made it possible for me to decently provide for you, Mary."

"It was a long time ago."

"Yes, but when I came back from school in New York, you were calling my mother mom. It broke my heart."

What was left unsaid was when my mom called great-grandma Pauline mom, it drove a wedge between my grandmother and her mother. A wedge that the three-year-old Mary couldn't have understood and one Gran couldn't forgive her mother for allowing for many years. I needed to change the conversation.

"Tell me about Dean Martin, Gran." We'd all heard the story a million times, but a million and one times was what this Christmas Eve needed.

"I twirled on the dance floor a couple of times with Dean. Had a drink or two with him before a couple of his shows, too. He sure brought the crowds in. But Dean was a man who needed a harem around him. A pretty boy, a damn pretty boy, with no reason to have morals at that time of his life. It was right before he hit the big time, and we were all there to see it. Back then he still felt most comfortable in his home town at one of the first clubs where he sang.

"It was that six-foot-four security guard with the wiry, scrubbing pad hair I noticed. I'd been the manager for about a year when I hired the security company he worked for. He only worked at night because he had another job with National Cash Register during the day. I saw him watching me, too, but I didn't want to be forward, not when I thought I might want to play for keeps. So I maneuvered Dean to introduce us.

"I was in Dean's dressing room when the security guard walked by. Dean said, 'Hey, tall rooster, can I introduce you to the most beautiful woman in this club, who just happens to manage it?'"

"Matt stopped and looked inside. There was another woman with blonde hair and me. He said, 'As long as it's the one with Scheherazade hair and eyes.'"

Gran still sighed like a school girl when she said that. In past years we all laughed when the story was finished, but this year we were silent as we remembered Matt.

We began opening presents, laughing and enjoying this special evening while Dean and Frank Sinatra continued to sing. After the last sweater was opened, I said, "Gran, there's one more present for you."

"Another one? Jake, you're too generous."

"Not as generous as you've been through the years. But, you have to find it." That was the clue she understood. With a big grin she nodded and began inching toward the edge of the couch so I could help her reach for the walker. Step-by-step, she headed toward the tree, looking like a hawk between the branches for what might still be left. Only a minute passed before she said, "I see it! I see it! Right there."

I leaned inside the branches and pulled out the present. She sat on a chair by the tree and held the box. I saw a tear fall on the cellophane, then another. "White Shoulders," she whispered, and I again heard Matt's voice from a memory twenty-three years ago to the day. "Let me tell you about my wife . . ."

Chapter 2

After all that, why is there more pain now?
MARY LEEANN STEWART BUCHANAN

December has all the Christmas magic of softly fall-ing snow, holly door wreaths and ribbon, and graceful trees laden with ornaments and tinsel. January has none of that. It is a forsaken month of dirty snow, too much football news, and little to celebrate. Lucky for Great Party! not everyone feels that way. There were a num-ber of football-watching parties, birthdays, office events, and of course, weddings. Why anyone would want to get married in January I don't know, but it keeps business steady.

On the third Saturday of the month we had three events: a secluded business annual meeting lunch for two dozen executives, and afternoon and an evening weddings.

I was busy making sure that the lavender napkins with "Tracy and Donald" stamped on them didn't get sent to Westridge's Corporate Meeting. From where I was I could see everything going on in the back. It was chaotic as people reached for tablecloths, stacked glasses, and lined up centerpieces. Everyone's movement looked like traffic racing in and out of lanes, trying to beat the lights.

A few minutes later I heard a crash. I rushed over to where the boy Logan had fallen. He was turned away from me, getting to his feet with Tim's help. I took his other arm to help him up and smelled liquor. Immediately I was angry. Event planning is not a business where there is room for an employee to be anything but alert and sure of his moves. My hold strengthened enough that Tim could feel it. He looked at me and let the kid go. I was ready to march Logan to my office and fire him.

But when I turned Logan around, I stopped. The whole left side of his face was bruised, starting with his black-rimmed, swollen eye that was not as open as the other. The bruise cascaded like veined granite down his cheek to a point of yellow nearing his chin.

"That didn't just happen," a teenage employee said. The kids, some horrified, others entertained, had gathered around.

"Everybody, back to work," Tim directed. "Lacey, Bernie, clean it up."

Logan shook his head, moving his long hair away from his face.

"Let's go to the office." I released my hold before turning and walking over crunching glass with him following.

Logan slunk into the chair against the wall, and I closed the door before walking to my chair behind the desk.

"What happened?"

"Nothing. Just fell."

"What happened?"

"Fell down some stairs. Stairs to the basement at home," his voice strengthened toward the end.

"What happened?"

He stared at his knees, but after a minute of silence he raised his right arm and ran it through his hair.

"Who hit you?"

"My mother's boyfriend."

I leaned back to think, and then got up and looked out the window at the dreary January day. Industrial parks are lifeless, ugly places on Saturdays. A mother's boyfriend. A father. Was there a difference in how it hurt? I almost lifted my hand to feel where my father had hit me when I was fifteen.

My father's ring, a weapon with a two-carat diamond set in twenty-four carat gold, left a gash, and the next day you couldn't tell the difference between the side of my head, nose or ear. While the doctor worked, my father had stood over me so I couldn't talk and tell how it really happened. Afterwards it hurt to run my tongue along the inside of my mouth. That injury was my punishment for being forty-five minutes late coming home.

I turned to look at Logan, "What else happened?"

"Nothing. My mom was there."

Mine hadn't been. I'd left my mother in Washington with my new stepfather two years earlier to live with my dad. I thought living with him would be better.

"Logan, I smell liquor on you."

He didn't deny it. I'd been drinking that night years ago. In fact, I'd been drinking most nights with my high school friends in that Steubenville, Ohio neighborhood. My father didn't care as long as I followed the little rules, like be home on time and show your stepmother respect. Respect was harder than being on time. She drank more than me and couldn't tell bologna from prosciutto.

"Listen, Logan, you know I should let you go. You know you can't drink and come to work. You can't."

He was still staring at his knees.

"But I'll cut you a little slack here. I think you're a good kid, just a mixed-up teenager." I took a breath and continued. "If you promise not to have anything to drink before you come to work, you can stay."

He sat up. "Okay."

"Okay, then you can go. Go home today. You've been drinking. You can come back for your next shift."

"Okay." He shuffled out of the room. I probably wouldn't have sounded any more grateful than Logan did if someone had been kind to me. It's not always easy to accept a little grace. Or even recognize it at the time. I remembered that, too.

Still, with over twenty part-time high school and college kids I couldn't have a problem child setting a precedent with bad behavior. I decided that if he came to work smelling of alcohol one more time, I'd fire him. He wasn't my responsibility.

I felt worn out. It was ten in the morning and I felt beat. I went to the back for a lemonade and sandwich from Chef Don before going back to the office to work on bids. Company growing pains meant mountains of paperwork.

I had come to work in the dark of a cold January morning and left in the dark of an early winter night. While I locked the door to leave, I thought of the one small bright spot my family always had in January. My mother's birthday was coming up in a few days on the twenty-third. As I drove up to the house I saw Shadow's nose resting on the windowsill as he waited for me. Shadow was not Liz, but he was a good welcoming committee.

"Anybody still up?" It was only after eight, but the house was quiet.

"I'm in here, Jake."

I followed Mom's voice to the living room. "Gran's already asleep?"

"She's in bed reading."

"I'll say good night."

I lightly knocked on the door and walked in. "Hi, Gran."

"Jake. Come sit down."

"What are you reading?"

"A love story, but it's not as good as mine."

"You and Matt had it all."

"Yes, we had it all."

After a few minutes I left her and went to the kitchen for something to eat. I expected Mom to be waiting for me at the dining table, but though the kitchen lights were on, she wasn't there. I figured she'd gone to her bedroom. I opened a can of soup and heated it in the microwave. I heard Shadow give a long low whimper.

"Shadow?" It was quiet. "Shadow?"

I heard my mom's voice from the living room. "He's in here, Jake. With me."

I went to her. "What are you doing sitting in the dark?"

"I don't know. I just needed to sit."

"What's wrong, Mom?" I sat down beside her.

"I'm just tired, Jake. It's nothing. Everyone gets tired."

The light from the kitchen was not on her, but I could see she had been crying. "Yes, but not everyone gets teary over it." I touched her cheek. "What's wrong?"

"After all my mother went through. After all that, why is there more pain now?"

"What do you mean?"

"You know. You've heard the stories. Why after her childhood, after what she went through when I was born, and the years after, why should there be even a minute's more pain?"

"I don't know." I put my hand on her shoulder. Shadow had his nose in Mom's lap. "It's been hard for you to watch her get weaker, hasn't it?"

"Oh, yes. And I don't know how much longer I'm

going to be able to get her up during the day when you're not here. And keeping her pills all straight is a daily math test. My back aches. Sometimes it's all I can do."

I didn't say anything. I felt powerless.

Then she spoke again. "Lately, I've even felt badly that I was born in January and made her walk all alone through all that snow."

"That wasn't your fault."

"No, but sometimes it feels like it. I certainly made life harder for her."

We talked for a while longer, remembering Gran's story of my mother's birth. Then she said she was too tired and wanted to go to bed, but I think she also wanted to go cry for a few minutes and just get the pain out. I rewarmed the soup and took it to my computer, intending to check up on a few social emails, but all I could do was stare at the screen.

Mom had looked tired as she shuffled out of the living room to her bedroom. Gran had looked tired, too. I knew I was. Logan, the quiet boy with the bruise on half his face, had looked weary of everything this morning. Anne's voice had an edge of exhaustion to it whenever I heard it. Only Liz's voice had the sparkle of life, an energy that lifted my spirits even when she was impatient and wanted to end our phone call to go meet her friends.

Liz needed protection. Protection from all the worries. All the doubts and fears and hurts and tragedies that life was made up of needed to be kept from her, so she could experience something else. What life could be. When I was her age I had felt like the most vulnerable, unloved, unvalued, lonely person in the world. My whole body sagged, and I felt momentarily defeated. How could I, a father two states away, protect her so she would not feel that way? How could I help her life be easier than her great-grandmother's, grandmother's and mine?

As usual, Gran and Mom were in the kitchen when I came in the next morning.

"Finish your book, Gran?" I asked.

"Not yet. Maybe today."

"We talked about you last night, didn't we Mom?"

"Only about the best parts," my mother said.

Gran smiled, "You should write it down, Jake. I don't want you to forget it."

"I couldn't forget you."

"You'd be surprised what you can forget if you try hard enough. I've forgotten all about that miserable night Mary was born."

"That's what we talked about," I said.

"I hope you didn't brag too much," Gran answered.

Later that morning, I got a call from Cameron Enterprises telling me that Great Party! had won their bid for the end of May. It would be my biggest job yet with over five hundred guests for a lunch that they were treating like a state dinner. It was a new product launch, and they wanted everything perfect with a four course meal and champagne under tents. The event was a huge undertaking, but I was ready and felt sure I could pull it off with the help of my staff and vendors.

The days started flying by with everything I needed to get accomplished completed. It was a good thing I had a strong staff and good relationships with my suppliers and vendors. Mom's birthday came and vanished in a tailwind. January was finally winding down, and I hoped February would bring sunnier days.

The first Friday of February I met Eric for a racquet-ball game. Afterward we went to a noisy place for dinner and then over to a popular bar, Voyeur, to meet Carly and her friends. I danced a few dances, but recovered alcoholics either get bored or start drinking again when people are headed to their third drink. I excused myself and went to my Audi to go home. The luxury car, with leather seats and enough technology to fly an airplane, had been my divorce present to myself purchased for the sole purpose of comforting a broken heart. As I pulled away, I saw the growing line waiting to get in the club. Under the street light I saw Logan. He was laughing in a huddle of three friends, their breath creating clouds that rose and disappeared. He had the goofy, slack face of someone who had already had too much to drink. He didn't see me and I turned away so he wouldn't.

Was that how I looked when I was his age? Probably. I know I tried as hard as it looked like he did to fit in with other kids. I would have been standing there in my 1980s unlaced high-tops with my skinny black jeans tucked into them, wearing a tee-shirt and a tight dress jacket. The preference for Depeche Mode, David Bowie, and George Michael may have changed, but not the face of cockiness masking fear and hurt.

I was still thinking of Logan when I got home and sat at the computer. I turned it on and leaned back to wait for the familiar screen. Logan was only a few years older than Liz. Oh, those years were dangerous, and I was so far away from her. How would I tell her? How would I warn her about the dangers? How would I make her understand that she had me and that under any circumstances she would always have me to depend on?

I stared at the screen until it darkened to screen-saver black. Liz needed to know her great grandmother's story and understand at least part of how she would have felt. I had to write it as best I could. I sat back to think for a few minutes, then woke the computer, put my fingers on the keyboard and began. At the top of the blank screen I typed my grandmother's name: Alwida Emerson Stewart Arnold, the date of my mother's birth, and then I began typing as if I had been my grandmother.

Chapter 3

Alwida Emerson Stewart
January 23, 1945
BAKERTON, PENNSYLVANIA

It was midnight when I felt the first pain. I hadn't fallen asleep, though I'd been trying to for an hour. I wanted sleep to use up the time that seemed stuck, not moving at all. The three quiet thumps on the inside of my belly felt like a mailman knocking on the door. They stopped and I tried to sleep, but by four o'clock I knew I couldn't. Why couldn't it all wait? Why couldn't everything just go back and let me figure things out?

I didn't want it. Not that way anyway. With the first break of day's grey light in the room, I couldn't stand it anymore so I got up. The other side of the bed hadn't been touched. I hadn't moved a toe into Clive's side. I hadn't disturbed the pillow or touched the bedspread. In the kitchen I got a glass of milk, but I could barely force down a swallow. I looked down at my swollen belly. It didn't feel like it belonged to me, and I didn't know what to think about what it held.

All morning I walked back and forth through the small bedroom, living room, and kitchen. I swept the floor and cleaned the kitchen sink. I warmed up canned chicken and rice soup, but I only ate three bites. I left the bowl on the table. Maybe I would want some later.

The pains were a little stronger, but not any more than a quick punch or two like Clive would give my arm in fun. He had to come home. About noon it started to snow tiny flakes that dissolved as they hit the ground. I sat on the couch to watch the snow and held a pillow against my stomach, trying to force everything to quiet down. I listened to the radio. Music always calms me. I wanted it to make the baby sleep again and not want to be born. It needed to wait with me until Clive got home. It hadn't started moving yet when I'd asked Clive not to go out, but I'd had a feeling. He was with his friends on Thursday night and he went out Sunday, too, and here it was Tuesday. I had asked him to stay with me.

I wanted to call my mother. She'd come. Maybe she'd be screaming and yelling "Hurry, hurry," or maybe she'd be crying and hugging while she called me her baby, but she'd come. Behind her would be Sam, my stepfather, who was the only dad I ever knew. He takes care of Mom, keeps her controlled, a little calmer. Sometimes she just lies in his arms like a rag doll and cries until she sounds like a hiccuping baby.

I remember when she was strong all the time. Maybe if I remember that, think really hard about that, the baby will be still and listen to the stories that will belong to it.

My mother, Pauline Gerard Emerson McAlister, was sometimes weak in her mind, but she was always strong in her arms and legs. She worked hard on her parents' few acres growing vegetables, keeping chickens, two cows, and always a few pigs. As an only child she followed both her parents around, and by the time she was a teenager she could run the farm herself. Even the still Grandpa had in the basement.

Mom was rooted on that small farm. Whatever life she had walked into, that plot of land demanded her attention. And then along came Frank Emerson.

Stooped and pulling weeds and early onions in mud-streaked overalls, she probably looked more like a young, slender boy than a woman to the man who walked over from the road to ask for work. She told me he looked like a big old lug nut, broad in the shoulders, skinny in the legs, with a head a good pounding couldn't hurt. He was the first man who paid attention to her and seemed plenty happy to settle in with her parents, a woman who knew how to put food on the table, and free rent. They married, I was born, and two years later he told her he wasn't meant for the easy life. He needed the grit of city.

By then the Depression had settled in and my grandparents were both weaker and needed help. They looked after themselves, but it was Mom who started running things. She was always busy gathering eggs, yelling at the neighbor kids who were hired to milk the cows, reminding her father to string up the beans, or put oil in the truck. Sometimes she'd hire one of the wandering, lost men without work who came to the porch for food to clean the barn or fix a fence. But usually she'd just set the sandwiches and a few apples on the back steps where they could take them. I had a red wagon Mom would fill with vegetables and eggs before sending me through the neighborhood to sell them. The Depression wasn't easy, but to a kid, it was just a life of work.

One day when I was five I was down in the fruit cellar watching the mash, reading dials, almost light-headed with the smell that mixed with damp walls, aging apples, and potatoes in burlap sacks. Two men came down dressed in suits and carrying hammers, but when they saw me they stopped and then smiled, wide as the monkey's smile I'd seen in a picture book. I told them the truth, "It's not ready yet."

"Oh, it's ready," the tall one said and sent me upstairs. For the next hour Mom and I stood in the hallway listening to Grandpa's voice from his upstairs bedroom. With every whack to his still by the government's men, Grandpa's cursing of prohibition was returned in equal measure.

I don't know how Mom and Sam met. I've never bothered asking. It seemed like he just sprouted out of the ground in the spring, around the time watercress lines the open ditch. He became a part of us, and he did make things better.

Where was Clive? Time that January afternoon wasn't moving, and the snow in the front yard began to thicken into white frosting. While I thought about my mother, the street turned white and the country road became invisible.

I knew Mom and Sam would come if I walked next door and called from the landlord's, but I didn't want them. I didn't want to be like them. My life was to be different. Even Sam said so. When I told Mom that Clive and I were getting married, she shrieked for Sam out the back door. In he ran, thinking she was having a heart attack. For an hour he tried to calm both of us as I insisted that I loved Clive, and Mom insisted that at seventeen I was too young to make that decision. There was no need to rush into marriage. Didn't I know about my own father?

That night Sam had stopped me in the hall when I tried to pass him to go to my room. "Alwida," his voice sounded tired like a rusty saw against wood "You can do better."

I just pushed past him. While living on a chicken farm in the middle of nowhere? I thought. Besides, Clive had promised he'd take me away from here. We'd talked about living a different kind of life without cows and pigs. One where we danced, played cards, and had dinners on white tablecloths with bone china and heavy silver. I wanted that life to start now.

Clive Stewart and I were married by the justice of the peace. We didn't have a fancy city wedding in our backward town of coal-mining dirt, but Mom had put on a good party at home. She tried to smile in happiness for me as she made the sandwiches, potato salad, and cake. The table did look beautiful with three vases of flowers, lace tablecloths, and blue plates. I stood with Clive wearing my white wedding gown, sure I was a princess with the most handsome, best dancer in Bakerton. All our cousins, aunts, and uncles toasted us and wished us the very best. I knew I was on my way to real life.

We lived with Mom and Sam for three months until I found the place the old couple owned. They lived on the other side of the wall in the duplex, and Clive did the maintenance and cut the lawn last summer. I cleaned for them and did their laundry. We celebrated our first anniversary here when I was five months pregnant.

Where was Clive? I was getting afraid. It had been sixteen hours since the first pain. It wasn't stopping. The pains were getting harder. I needed the hospital.

The man on the radio said roads were closing down. It looked like it would be to my knees if I went outside. Evening was beginning to silence the world, and the snow looked so pretty. I couldn't hear a car or see a single one on the street. There was only the old couple next door.

Nat King Cole played on the radio, and I knew his

voice wasn't going to cover my cries much longer. There wasn't going to be any more time. I needed help. My suitcase was packed and sitting by the wall in the bedroom. I had packed a robe, nightgown, slippers, and a bottle of nail polish. I put my toothbrush and tooth powder in to finish the packing and got my coat—a brown wool "practical" thing. It was ugly and plain with a Peter Pan collar, but it was all Arlene's Dresses had left when Mom went shopping for Christmas last year. She said that now that I was married I needed to be practical. She thought it was nice. I swore never to own another brown winter coat as long as I lived, unless it was mink. Where was my hat? I got down on my knees and bent over my whale belly before I saw it on the floor. I couldn't put on the gloves. My hands were swollen. I was fat and swollen at nineteen.

I knocked on the old couple's door, at first lightly, but they didn't hear so I knocked harder. They needed to answer the door. The snow was falling straight down, without wind, so I was out of it on the porch. The light finally went on.

"Hello, Mr. Janssen. I'm sorry to ask you this, but I need to. Could you see your way to drive me to the hospital?" My suitcase was by my feet. Mrs. Janssen came up behind him, and when she saw it was me she waved him aside.

"Let her in, Derek, let her in. Poor child, we can wait for tomorrow for any cleaning."

"She wants a ride to the hospital."

Kindly Mrs. Janssen stopped and looked at the snow. "Then we need to take her."

While they got their coats and rubber boots I sat on the couch. When Mr. Janssen went outside to start the car I had another pain, but I muffled my hurting voice into the sleeve of my coat and hoped their deafness would keep it from them.

When we were in the old 1940 coupe I saw the old couple look at each other before Mr. Janssen backed out. I'd never seen a couple look like that at each other. Full as a book of meaning without a word. They wondered if they were going to get me to the hospital. The snow came to the bottom of the car even on the road. No one else was driving. I wondered where Clive was hiding away from the snow. Was he having fun, or could he be walking home, cold and afraid I wasn't okay?

We drove in silence for two miles, all three of us equally frightened and awed by the snow. We nearly slid off twice, but since we were the only ones on the street, Mr. Janssen drove in the center of the road. The snow was deeper closer to the hospital. When we came to the edge of town, there was a push on the front of the car. The snow was fighting the coupe harder. Mr. Janssen pushed on the gas. The back end fish-tailed a slow, lazy sway.

He stopped. "It's not far, Alwida."

"Yes, Mr. Janssen." I scooted to the door, held my suitcase and got out. The way we had come was the only way there was over country road, but there was still a mile to go. I walked in the light of the headlights until they faded as Mr. Janssen backed up before turning around.

The quiet was not like life. I'd never heard this kind of silence. My boots did not make noise. Neither did the snow. The absence of sound made the baby move. This time I did not hold back. A wrenching, painful sound came from me that I would have thought was an animal's, but I felt it vibrate. I felt it through my whole body. I had to think. I had to make it to the hospital. I couldn't die out here for something that didn't know it wasn't time. Didn't know its daddy wasn't here. Was this how having a baby was supposed to be?

I remembered when Sam had started coming by to see mother. He brought me licorice and another time a hand mirror. He said I was the prettiest little girl he'd ever seen. After they got married, Mom got pregnant and had a baby at this hospital I'm walking to, but it never came home. And she was never the same. That's when Sam started to stroke her hair and say, "Pauline, it's not that bad. Really, it's not that bad." After a while I wondered if she even remembered why she cried. It was so long ago.

The mile was almost walked. My left hand was stuck to the suitcase. Now came the stairs that went up the back way to the hospital. As kids we used to play on them. Clive was part of the crowd, but not very often. He was three years older and would only come around to tease the rest of us, daring us to jump across and fall down them. But I had never counted them. I looked up. The lights of the hospital were just beyond.

At fifty steps I couldn't tell how far I needed to go. At seventy-nine I stopped and bent over in pain, howling. At one hundred-eight I put my cold hand on my sweating, hot forehead. At one hundred-eighteen I couldn't tell through the snow that there was only one more step. I walked into the hospital's front door looking like a snowman with my belly bulging out from a brown coat covered in snow, and then I fell.

When I woke the next day, I looked around to see three other women in beds and two empty beds at the end of the room. I felt my now soft belly and vaguely remembered a few moments of bright lights when a nurse was holding a baby in front of me and said, "You have a girl." Someone had rolled me away to the darkness of this room. I turned my head and saw a window. There was blue sky and the tops of trees from the one hundred-nineteen step height of the hospital. At 11:00 a.m. Clive walked in the room. Three women stared at him, one was asleep. Through smell of the bleached sheets by my face, I smelled sour whiskey.

He looked at me like I was a ghost. I felt like one.

"It's a girl" I said.

He nodded, got a chair by an empty bed, brought it over and sat down. He was pale.

"I was at George's. Then it started snowing." His black hair was perfectly combed and glistened in hair cream.

"I've got a name for her."

"Yeh?"

"Mary. Mary LeeAnn. It has a nice, smooth sound like a love song."

He promised to tell my parents and come get me when it was time to go home. As I watched him leave I wondered if this was how my mother felt when I was born and when the other one died.

It was after midnight when I turned the computer off and headed to my bedroom. There was a strange mixture of elation and dread in my chest from trying to tell my grandmother's story.

The next night I made excuses to leave Mom and Gran early and head to the computer. I felt driven to at least finish this chapter.

Gran wasn't happy with me. "What are you doing on that thing? It takes you away from people. I'm glad we didn't have them when I was your age. I would have missed the best years of my life and so will you!"

"Sleep well, Gran," I said. "See you in the morning."

Two hours after Clive left the hospital that January morning so long ago, Mom and Sam walked in the room. The nurse had made them wait half an hour until the proper visiting time after lunch. The love and peace that flooded my mother's face when she first held Mary frightened me. Maybe I shouldn't say that, but now I know a little about why it did and back then I didn't. I just knew it frightened me.

"When Clive gets you home, we'll bring dinner over won't we, Sam?" my mother said.

"Yes."

"I'm going out this afternoon to buy a dress for little Mary, too. A pretty, frilly dress that will be made for a princess. And I'll make pink sleepers. You'll need them."

"I'm coming home Saturday."

"I'll make a pot roast and then you'll have leftovers. I'll make a pie. What kind do you want?"

"I don't feel like eating."

"You will. Banana cream pie has always been your favorite. I'll make that."

"Thanks, Mother."

When he led Mom out Sam was smiling too. He always liked to see her happy. I hoped to be happy.

The next few weeks were a blur. I hurt for a good week. I thought once a baby was born it wasn't supposed to hurt, but it did. I felt torn apart from my stomach and right through the top of my head. And Clive wasn't happy about any of it. He didn't like how my stomach looked, that the doctor told him he had to leave me alone for a few weeks, that the baby cried, and I didn't make very good meals, and the house was dirty. It was all I could do to care for the baby and then go knock on Mr. and Mrs. Janssen's door to clean their bathroom and wipe up the kitchen floor.

The first week he stayed around. I think he felt a little guilty like he was supposed to be a good dad, but he didn't know what to do. His muscled arms looked like stiff tree branches that didn't know how to bend when he tried to hold Mary. And the look he gave her was as much fear as some kind of surprise, like "How in the hell did I do this?" He wasn't working steady, but a local freight company paid him to be an extra delivery man on call, and he sometimes helped an uncle who laid linoleum and wood floors. He kept the payments up on the car, paid for his nights out, and sometimes put grocery money on the kitchen table. Sam handed me a few dollars every time he came over with Mom.

I had my energy back before March, but there was so much more to do. Mom visited almost every day, and Clive's mom came a few times, but still there was a lot more to do than I expected.

Clive wasn't touching me much. When we first went out he couldn't keep his hands off me. He loved how soft and smooth I was. He said I smelled good and I made him feel strong. I loved his broad shoulders and how the pleated pants went straight down from his hips.

We started calling Mary "the baby." Her eyes had focused, and she gazed at me like a new kitten when I breast fed her or changed her diapers. I was confused.

I didn't understand how I felt. I would feel so tired and when I looked down at that little face my heart felt like a wrench turning a bolt. I couldn't tell if the tightness meant love, fear, or anger.

The baby and I went out with Clive a couple of times on Wednesday nights or Sunday afternoons to his cousin's house or to sit around at George's. Before the baby I would sometimes sit at the table with the men and a few of the other girls, but now I was supposed to stay on the couch and talk to the girls who stayed in there. Mine was the only baby.

I always wondered if I hadn't complained that Friday when he put the five dollars on the kitchen table if things would have turned out different. He'd worked the day with his uncle, and when he came in the door he looked like a creature out of a movie with the fine spray of sawdust all over him. "Only five dollars? How much did he pay you to look like that?"

"None of your business." His voice had such venom I shut up. He cleaned up and didn't look at me when he walked out the door all fresh and smelling of cologne. Monday morning he came home and the first thing he did was tell me to sit down.

"I'm going to California to find work. There's better work there."

"When?"

"Soon."

"What kind of work?"

"Better work. I don't know. Maybe in the movies."

"I want to go, too."

"No, Alwida, no."

We stared at each other. "What?" This was not going to be. I couldn't be left here. No. It went on for an hour until my anger turned to pleading. I promised the baby and I wanted to go and we wouldn't be any trouble. He finally stood, looking tired and half hung over and then he left again. At the end of the day he was back with a few more dollars and he slept so deeply his snores woke the baby. We argued whenever he was home, but it was useless. He always ended my pleas to go with him by going to sleep, walking out the door, or saying, "There isn't room for you."

The fight wasn't any different the Wednesday morning when he left for good. At least I didn't think it was any different until three days passed. And then a fourth and a fifth. When Mom visited I didn't say anything. It was always daytime and she was accustomed to Clive being away. Her visits were only long enough to hold the baby, change a diaper, and put her back in the crib. Then she had to leave to finish the planting, go to the feed store, or fix dinner. So I waited.

I started eating less and by the seventh day the only food I had left were bottled peaches and tomatoes from Mom, potatoes, and half a pound of hamburger Mrs. Janssen gave me when I went over on the fifth day to clean. When Mom stopped by, I didn't let her know anything was wrong. Mrs. Janssen let me use the telephone to call George.

"Hi George, I want to talk to Clive." The silence let me know.

"I haven't seen him for days, Alwida."

"Oh. Well, when you see him, let him know."

"Yeh."

I felt hollow and alone. For the next two days all I did was listen to the radio and take care of my baby. I didn't turn on the lights once. The drapes were closed. I didn't get dressed or comb my hair. When Mr. Janssen knocked on the door I didn't answer. My life felt ended. The baby and I were two outcasts who lived in a cave. On the tenth day all I had left was a bottle of peaches.

When the baby went down for her morning nap, I took a long bath and washed my hair. For the first time since she was born I did my nails in Siren Red. Then I packed our clothes. I walked next door to use the telephone and when Sam answered I told him Clive was gone; he went to California to find work. They were over to get Mary and me within the hour.

Over the next days my mother cried every time the baby cried. She told me I should have a few tears in me, but I told her that she and the baby were doing all the crying that place could stand. I had plans. I stayed until I'd earned enough money through odd jobs to buy three dresses. On the morning I left, I went into the nursery Mom and Sam had made. I kissed the baby's small perfect cheek and stroked her dark hair. "I've got to go, Mary LeeAnn, but I know you'll be taken care of, and I have to do this."

I picked up the suitcase I'd left by the back door, kissed my mother good-bye and left with Bob for the bus station and secretarial school in New York.

Chapter 4

"What did you bring me to, Matthew?
This is a hellhole!"

ALWIDA ARNOLD

As dreary as February is, it's an improvement on January. Snow still has a winter heft under a snowplow, and temperatures are just as bitter, but the days get a touch brighter and longer even through snowstorms. My days raced by with all I had to do to keep up with the parade of Super Bowl parties, business retreats that needed boxed lunches, store openings, and weddings. Finally the years of suffering it takes to start a business were beginning to pay off with referrals and return customers.

I was considering hiring another person, but I wasn't sure if I should make it a sales position so I would have more time, or a management position that crunched the numbers and oversaw operations so I could continue the sales. Doing both was getting to be too much. Plus, I knew it wouldn't be long before Tim would need extra help. With all the duties he had to pull an event together, it would soon be overwhelming.

The increase in business meant he handled a larger pool of part-timers. There was a time I knew all our employees, but now they came and went like the falling snow. One person after another passed through, trying to make a little extra money. I'd seen Logan a few times, once or twice by chance, and another time intentionally when I stood by him for a good look in his eyes to make sure he was clean. He was, so I let him by.

One Wednesday night the truck came back at midnight to unpack from a wedding. I went out to help unload serving plates, linen, a few containers of sandwiches and pasta salad that looked pretty limp at that hour.

Logan and I caught eyes, which was not easy with his heavy eyebrows and thick, dark hair. It fell around his face after being loosened from the ponytail and net he'd worn during the party. There I was at seventeen. A tight jaw. Eyes that were equally surly bravado and pleading innocence.

As he left I saw him pick up a leftover container of finger sandwiches and an aging banana before heading out the door into twenty degree weather. I let the kids take leftover food when they got back so that wasn't unusual, but I'd told Tim not to use high schoolers that late on a school night.

"Tim, why was that kid Logan on tonight? He's younger."

"Yeah, I know, but I think he's dropped out of school. He called me about two this afternoon and begged to be put on, and I wasn't sure I'd have enough help so I gave in."

It was either lost kids without futures who wanted to work here or future rocket scientists working their way through the university. Sometimes I hoped one would learn from the other as they worked, but the college ones could be real snots to the high schoolers.

A few days later I was at my desk creating a more detailed timetable for the Cameron job when the phone rang. "Great Party! Jake here."

"Is Mr. Buchanan in?"

"This is Jake. How can I help?"

"This is Hillside High. Logan Norris is a student here. He's been absent a few days and I'm trying to locate him. I understand he is an employee with your company. Is that right?"

"Yes, he is."

"Is he there now?"

"No, we don't have high schoolers in the morning."

"I see. Well, he hasn't been in school since last week. When you see him, will you tell him to call and come back to school. He shouldn't jeopardize his student status any longer."

"Yes. Yes, I will."

That afternoon when I knew the day's crew would be in, I went into the back. Tim was away picking up linens and I didn't see Logan, so I walked over to two other workers, Todd and Melissa, who I'd seen with him.

"Hey."

"Hey, Mr. Buchanan." They both stopped wrapping cookies and watched me.

"Have you seen Logan?"

"Not today," said Todd.

"Is he in school?"

"He went last week."

"Is he in school?"

Todd had been answering, but with the silence Melissa chimed in. "Not much. He's been having trouble at home."

"Next time you see him tell him the school called here and he needs to go."

It only took a minute to block Logan out of my mind. I had enough going on that day. I hadn't remembered his last name until the woman on the phone said it. Over an hour later the crew was getting ready to leave when Melissa's head appeared around the door. She sighed and gathered her strength before standing fully in the doorway.

"Yes?"

"Mr. Buchanan, Logan's in the homeless shelter. He spends his days looking for work and sitting in the library. He's not in school." Then she was gone to get in the truck.

Bosses don't want to know everyone's personal life. A well-run business can't be worried about personal lives too. Frustrated about having more information than I wanted, I turned and looked out the window to calm myself down. Snow was starting to line the streets, inching in on the four-lane black asphalt road in front of Great Party!

The night's one event was over early and the trucks and crew returned before nine. Three inches of snow was on the top of one of the trucks when it pulled in the garage and I went to help unload it. After locking the back door and hearing only the crunch of my feet on snow as I walked, I sat in my cold car. My breath fogged up the window in front of me, but I just sat there. A streetlight sent its yellow length of light through the passenger window.

I remembered the old red truck's windows had fogged almost as soon as Pap, Gran, and I had sat in it that late afternoon. The Christmas tree I'd just cut was on the top, tied by three ropes Pap and I had secured. Gran spread a napkin on her lap to protect her clothes while she poured the coffee and hot chocolate. Pap started the truck and slowly eased it forward through the snow, and Gran leaned over to do the shifting from first to second since Pap's arm was weakened from broken ribs.

"Wave at Lawrence, Jake. Matt can't," she said.

I opened the window, leaned out and gave Lawrence a big wave. He didn't know how much I had to thank him for and maybe he never would. That day changed my life, but at that moment, all I knew was I was happy. Happy for the first time since I could remember. Over the next hour we drove through the wonderland of a Washington snowfall, nearly losing our way past dairy farms and bare winter orchards on our way back to my grandparents' home in Bothell, Washington.

On this snowy February night over twenty years later, I started my car and waited the one or two minutes today's cars need to warm up. I got out and wiped the snow off the windows, still thinking about what to do, but by the time I got in the car, I'd made up my mind.

There are at least three homeless shelters in downtown Salt Lake that take in anyone who needs a bed. They were in the same neighborhood so I could cruise by each one. I wasn't going inside. If I saw him outside, fine.

The line of men was a scraggly sad thing to see. Over to the side was a line of women with children which was worse to see, though their line was shorter. At the second shelter on Second South I slowed as best I could to look through the dark figures for a suffering teenager. Men held blankets over their heads, a few had hoods, and other heads were bare. Three men looked like they were arguing. In front of them was a gap, perhaps deliberately created to separate from the others. And there was Logan, moving up to be closer to the men in front of him. A car was coming up behind, but I stopped and touched the automatic roll down on the passenger window.

"Hey, Logan." I yelled it twice, but he didn't hear me. The car came up behind and gave a short honk before going around, but Logan still didn't look up. Ahead I saw a three-minute passenger zone and pulled over. He didn't see me until I was standing a foot away in front of him. His eyes changed from sad to unreadable in a second.

"Your school called."

He shrugged his shoulders and took a step as the line moved up.

"I heard you've been living here."

"Don't fire me, Mr. Buchanan."

"I'm not here to fire you. I, uh, I . . . come with me. You need a meal."

He huddled deeper into himself, seeming to shrink to a twelve-year-old.

"Come with me. It'll be quieter." He moved another step in line.

I know you're not supposed to do these things for a hundred good reasons. Labor laws, child protection laws, protect your own privacy common sense, but I did. I took his arm and led him away. For a boy who said no, he was surprisingly easy to lead.

We didn't talk at all on the twenty minute drive to my house. As we pulled in the driveway I said, "I live with my mother and grandmother." He followed me in like a scared puppy.

Shadow barked, but soon stopped, appearing as troubled by the kid's appearance as I was. Calling him a wet noodle would be complimentary. He was more of a limp, discarded scrap.

"Mom, Gran, if you're still up, I've got company." I

heard the television.

"Company? For heaven's sake, Jacob, I'm in my robe!" Mom walked in the kitchen and stopped.

"I bet he's hungry" I said. "Have we got any food? Hungry, Logan?"

"I've got, well let me see, we have leftover roast and potatoes. Green beans. Want that? Or I can make a tuna sandwich with canned soup," Mom said.

"Logan?"

"Roast and potatoes."

As Mom warmed up the food, I pointed to the table for Logan to sit. Shadow sat on his hind legs staring at him.

Then around the corner came Gran silently moving her walker along the carpet on quiet little feet. Her hair was still combed, her dress still the flowing full length day dress she liked to wear. "I heard someone say we had a guest."

"You didn't need to get up, Gran."

"She wasn't asleep, Jake, only reading," Mom said.

Along the kitchen floor her walker made a sliding sound as she made her way to the table. "Oh, a young man. How nice, and he looks just like you did when you came home from Ohio, Jake. Is he yours?"

"My employee, Gran, and you don't need to tell him all the family stories."

"He looks unable to hear at the moment. A little dazed I'd say, like he saw a raccoon coming out of the fireplace. And dirtier than he should be."

"Mother!"

"Have you ever seen a raccoon come running out of the fireplace young man? I have and what's your name?"

"This is my grandmother, Logan. Her name's Alwida. His name's Logan, Gran."

I had moved the chair, making it easier for her to sit at the head of the table. "Logan, huh? That's a western name. You'd never hear that back in Steubenville. You haven't said anything. What's your last name, Logan?"

"Here's some food, Logan," Mom said setting the plate in front of him.

"Uh, Norris."

"Norris. That's a little better. I'll tell you about the raccoon."

"Go ahead and eat. This will take a few minutes." I sat at the other end.

"I wasn't sure about that house at all. It was a wreck and looked like it would always be a wreck, but my husband Matt loved the barn, loved the acre and a half it sat on with fruit trees and pines and aspens. It had a split rail fence in front. So I let him talk me into living in a motor home in the driveway for six months while he fixed it up. Go ahead, eat, Logan, you look so skinny you might become invisible tonight if you don't just vanish. Whoosh!

"Anyway, Matt was in the kitchen measuring for new kitchen cabinets. He made them from start to finish, best fitting cupboards you ever had in a kitchen anywhere. He had me working in the living room doing some fool thing to keep me out of his way when I heard a noise, a scream like an alley cat held by its tail, and when I turned around a raccoon was bounding from the fireplace, nearly as dirty as you, racing for the door. I let out a scream, and Matt came rushing in right passed that critter who beat it out the back door. 'What did you bring me to, Matt? This is a hellhole!' I said.

"'It's alright, Willie, it's alright,' he says to me in that way he always did. I think it was that day I went into the kitchen, not two hours later and humph! My leg went right through those rotten floorboards. He turned from his measuring to see me with one leg in the kitchen and one in a basement of killer spiders."

Logan must have been picturing all this as he inhaled the food because a smile started across his face.

"'Matt', I said, mad now, 'you better take me to the hospital for tetanus. How could you bring me to this house?'" She stopped and her voice changed. "It was a miracle the way he did put that house together. Wasn't it, Jake?"

"Yes, Matt was handy with a hammer."

"And a saw, a measuring tape, sander, anything you put in the man's hands."

"Every Friday, Logan, this is the miracle," she leaned over and put her old skinny fingers on his hand. He didn't flinch, which surprised me. "Every Friday for all the years we were married he had a dozen red roses sent to me."

She leaned back and Logan broke the silence. "That's real nice, Mrs. Buchanan."

"Mrs. Arnold, Logan, Mrs. Arnold. But you can call me Ms. Alwida."

Eighty-four years was showing on her stamina, but she continued. "Well, the house turned out to be beautiful, but like Dean Martin would sing, 'In the misty moonlight, by the flickering firelight, anyplace is all right, long as I'm with you,'" She made a move to get up from her chair, so I helped her up and we headed to her bedroom.

When I got back I said, "Have you got friends you can stay with, Logan? I can drive you there."

Surprised, Mom turned and looked at me like I'd said the wrong thing. Luckily, Logan was looking down, and I shot her a look to be quiet.

"Not really."

"No one?"

"I could call Todd."

"Try him." He used our phone and shuffled through a muffled conversation I tried not to hear, though I heard a note of pleading, and a pause before he hung up.

"I can go to Todd's."

"Let's go."

My last words to him as he got out of the car were, "Go to school."

Chapter 5

"And do you remember Klair, our 'Good Time Gal?'"
Alwida Arnold

It was during the last week of February when I had to cup my hands over the phone and talk directly into it because I knew my voice was rising, and if I wasn't careful, everyone in the back would hear my anger. "Listen, Ann, I don't know what your hang-up with that box is, but I've looked for it at least three times and it isn't there. It isn't there. Do you hear me?"

She heard me all right. She went into a full-tilt tantrum about me, the marriage, being forced to live in Salt Lake, and on and on. There wasn't going to be a return to a normal conversation, so I said goodbye and told her to call back when she was rational. Then I hung up.

It was a slower week for Great Party! There were only a handful of events, which gave me time to work more on Cameron Enterprises and a few other events, but it didn't prevent me from worrying about next month's payables. Around noon I walked back to get something to eat. "Hey, Don, that smells good," I said.

"Boeuf bourguignon," he said with a French flair, "for tomorrow. A night of resting will do it good, bring out the flavor."

"What do you think of the Cameron menu?"

"It needs tweaking. Can you get them to forget October's carrot cake and go with something more springy? Like strawberry lemon cake or raspberry cheesecake?"

"I'll get you in on the next meeting. How are things back here going otherwise?" I began making a sandwich.

"Jake, I need to let you know something I overheard the kids talking about. It may not be anything, but here it is."

"Yeah?"

"You know that little group that hangs together, Todd, Melissa, and Logan?"

"Yes."

"Yesterday afternoon while they were packing flatware I heard them talking. It seems that Logan's been visiting your house. He mentioned your grandmother. Is her name Alwida?"

I stopped spreading mayonnaise. "Yes."

"Well, he's been visiting her. I don't know how often."

"Is Logan working today?"

Don looked at a schedule thumb tacked on a board, "No. None of them are."

Oh, great, I thought as I headed back to the office with the sandwich. That's all I need.

I made a point of getting home before Gran had time

to go to sleep. This had to be stopped and why hadn't Mom said anything? They were eating dinner when I arrived. It's too easy to snack and taste at the office, so I wasn't hungry. I sat down with a purpose.

"Nice to have you at dinner, Jake," Mom said slightly sarcastically.

"All right you two conspirators. I've been told Logan's been coming around. What's the story?"

"Don't get me started, Jacob. His visits have to be," Gran said.

When Gran says "Don't get me started," I've learned to settle in a chair, buck up and enjoy the ride. She was already started. Sarcastic or not, Mom looked concerned for me.

"He needs us, Jake. There's no negotiation. Remember that waitress you grandfather called Tits McGee at the Seabird Café? If we hadn't heard how desperate she and her children were, we wouldn't have known she needed help. It was Matt who said, 'Willie, we've got to help,' and we did, even if she did wear her skirts so short you could almost see her stretch marks. If it hadn't been that Matt made those wooden pull toys, and we gave her some money after the divorce, her kids wouldn't have had a Christmas. Remember?"

I could only sigh.

"And do you remember Klair, our 'Good Time Gal'?"

"Yes." Who could forget Klair, a Realtor in the same office as Gran in Washington. She drove a yellow

Cadillac, wore rings on every finger, and had hair the size and shape of a hot air balloon. Matt called her a "Good Time Gal," but he didn't object when Gran gave her a couple of her real estate commissions so she could make it when her husband left her, even when she showed up for work half hung over. Grief and anger have many faces.

"Then I won't remind you how she paid for your tuxedo for the school dance once she got herself back on her feet."

"But Gran, Logan is an employee. I have to keep work separated from my life."

"Klair was a Realtor under me. The word employee doesn't mean they aren't human. And what about Lawrence?"

How was I going to take on Gran about Logan? I'd never forget Lawrence Heard. He was the man Gran had told me to wave to because Pap couldn't. He owned the tree farm where we cut the Christmas tree that day. Pap and Gran walked ahead while he stayed back and told me how my grandparents had saved his life and pointed the way to buying his own tree farm. He was part of what saved my life.

"Gran, laws have changed since then. Employers can't do certain things for employees. Especially underage ones."

"Then don't be here when he comes by. You haven't yet. I enjoy his company and he needs me. Like you needed me."

Mom flinched at this. It was a prick to her conscience from a long ago time.

"What do you talk about? I have a right to know that. I don't want every family story floating around work."

"Don't worry. I've sworn him to secrecy. You need to know his story isn't so different from yours. He's been living with his mother and her boyfriend, but the boyfriend isn't so great and for all I know, his dad wasn't much better. But he's dead. Two years ago. See?"

I got up to go relax away from these two. "Just keep it simple, okay?"

"We're chaperoned you know. Your Mom's here." Her grin could still win her Miss Congeniality. Logan was now an official problem. Bringing him home for a meal showed that one good act can be your downfall.

The clock said 2:17 a.m. when I woke from the dream. I don't remember all of it but I do remember what it was about. I thought that maybe if I exorcised it by writing it would leave, sort of like exposing something to fire so it burns away. Once the monsters were real on paper maybe I would lose some of the fear I knew was still chasing itself as residual tension and heartache in my body. I got up. The chill of the house would keep me awake. I wrapped myself in an old blue blanket Mom had put at the foot of the bed. When I sat at the computer, the screen light felt like an inquisitor. There is no lying to yourself in the deep of night.

This story wouldn't be my grandmother's. It was mine and my mother's. It was a time when I'd only heard of Gran and Matt in passing conversations. They lived in Reno and never visited us.

My first years were in Steubenville, Ohio where I lived with my mother and father, Pete Buchanan. Our house was thirty-five hundred square feet and always felt big to me. Its three split-level floors balanced on each other like a deck of cards shuffled by a child. Sometimes I played with a few kids in the neighborhood. During the day we'd ride our bikes along the streets, and in the long summer twilights we'd play chasing games in the wide adjoining yards without fences. When I was alone Mr. Jarsevick let me play in his greenhouse down the block. All our parents had to do to keep track of us was look out the window, or up from the newspaper while they sat on their back patio. But most of my time was spent in the kitchen with my mother where we'd watch a small television on the counter while she cooked or cleaned, and I ran cars and small fire engines along the counter top. In my bedroom I had a few books and toys, and I spent a lot of time working on puzzles in magazines Mom would get me when she went to the grocery store. Though it was never said out loud, the living room belonged to my father.

The living room at the back of the house leading to

the patio was his main reception area for guests. When he wasn't there, the stillness of the green, damask covered couch, wing back chairs, and glass coffee table with wrought iron legs, were a photo, an impossible space to step into. Outside the sliding glass doors, the patio furniture around a swimming pool was his summer reception area. Beyond, encompassing, were acres of lawns with houses spaced like soldiers.

When my father was there other men often came and went, sometimes for five minutes when bank receipts or piles of nickels, dimes, and quarters changed hands, and sometimes for five hours as they watched ball games on television. I got to know their faces and most of their names, but they weren't there to acknowledge me.

It was a sultry, heavy, summer day when Mom told me to dress in my suit I'd worn only to church. The starched cuffs of the white shirt chaffed on my wrist, but they weren't any stiffer than the cuffs my father had on his shirt. His business was a string of coin-operated laundries around the state named Pete's Laundries. He'd buy any small, run-down, one story building in a neighborhood with a lot of apartments, rip out whatever was in there, paint it yellow, and put in fifteen washer and dryer sets with a Coke machine. Once a sign was slapped over the front door, he was in business.

"Very good," was my father's high compliment when I met him in the hall wearing my suit. He towered above Mom and me, and was built rounded and strong like a cement truck. He had curly hair he kept short, molasses brown eyes, and big, always clean hands with rings on three fingers.

"You remember Florin who comes by, don't you? The guy who never matched his tie and suit, who collected the money in the south end of the state?" he asked when the two of us were in the car.

"Yes," my mother said.

"Well, he's not coming by again. Florin was in Athens in the Richland's store. He was pulling the money out of the third washer on the right when he had a heart attack. He wasn't found until the next morning. We're going to pay respects."

Larousse's Funeral Home was a two centuries old mansion set on a rolling hill. Inside we walked over a creaking wood floor, worn Persian carpet, passed tufted chairs by tables of dark wood and leather embossed insets. In a room beyond, was the casket of the first person I'd ever seen dead.

My father made me pay my respects to the bald man I had barely known lying in the casket. The roses and gladiolus were stacked four deep on three sides and their smell rose in an assault. The last time I'd seen Florin was a month before. He'd come to the house and Father took him through the hall, dining room, and living room before going out the sliding glass door to talk privately in front of the pool. When he came back through the house Florin seemed smaller than when he'd come. He walked fast and didn't look at Mom or me.

"See that spray, Jake?" my father said pointing to a four foot high arrangement of roses, gladiolus, and flowers I didn't recognize. "I sent that. He deserved it."

Most of the time my father was gone. He'd get up after I'd gone to school and come home as I was going to bed or after I was asleep. I didn't really know what he did when he was gone and I never asked. When the kids at school would talk about their dads being lawyers or plumbers, I would say my dad did laundry. When they stopped and stared at me, I'd add, "He's Pete's Laundry." They always recognized that name.

I've been asked if I was afraid of him and the answer has always has been, "No." What I did feel for my father, even as a child, was respect of space and power. He reigned in his home and with the men who worked for him. They were also his friends.

I liked it when he was away. Mom and I would go downstairs to the family room and watch shows like Charlie's Angels or Laverne and Shirley, and eat popcorn or cookies. Sometimes we went to dinner at different restaurants where he didn't like the food when she knew he wasn't going to be home.

With just Mom and me our house was quiet, but when he was there it was quieter. I learned to stay out of my dad's way unless he wanted me there. When he yelled, "Jake," saying the word like it was a stop signal for a train, I'd near run to him. Usually he wanted to show me something on TV like a boxing match or football game, and I'd sit with him to watch it, grateful for the warmth of some affection. Sometimes he called for me to get Mom from the yard because he wanted her to do something, and once he wanted me to dial a phone number and hand him the phone because he didn't want to get up.

I never questioned my relationship with my father. That was what fathers were like, I was sure. This was my world and I accepted it with nothing to compare it to.

I don't remember the beatings ever happening before I was seven. When I came back from a Saturday afternoon birthday party, I heard my mother screaming and my dad yelling, "Shut up, bitch." I ran up the stairs and stood shocked to stillness at seeing my mother on the floor with blood trickling down her cheek. Her eyes were closed and she began moaning. My father kicked her in the side, and her eyes jerked open unseeing. Then he saw me. His eyes were alive with a light I came to know held power, alcohol, disgust, and lust.

"Get out of here." His voice was so deep I felt it through my chest. My body was gathering fear. "Close the doors."

I closed the double French, glass-paned window doors and went to my room to stand in the center without moving. There weren't any more sounds that day. The beatings didn't happen often, at least I don't think they did. Maybe there were more than I remember and I'm making them melt together, hoping they will simmer, then burn away, at last taking the fear and leaving me free.

That first beating and the last two are the ones I clearly remember, and I can recite them like I'm reporting them to police right now. That's the only way to report them. They cannot be told with emotion because watching beatings cleans a person of emotion.

The next to the last beating of my mother was different. It happened in the family room while the news played on television. Father had come home angry and was mad his dinner wasn't hot when he walked in the door. Mom warmed it up, and while he ate he yelled about what some men had done. He sounded a little drunk, but I knew he wasn't as drunk as he could get on Sunday afternoons while watching football.

Mom made the mistake of leaving the kitchen before he was finished because she wanted to come down and watch television with me. Before she was halfway down the six stairs, he was up from the table and following her until he was close enough to kick her in the small of the back. She fell down the stairs.

"I've had enough today! Somebody's going to listen to me!"

Mom started crawling toward me.

"That's right, sit on that couch. Go to Jake. See what good it will do. Would you like to see what my day was like?" Then he started talking about "his" men, a building sale that failed, somebody that didn't tell the truth, and missing money. Ten minutes later he stopped, turned to look at us, and said, "This is what happened to me, today." He reached his right hand inside his suit coat, over to his left side where he drew out a small handgun, pointed it at us and fired. I didn't realize what had happened until it had passed between our heads and ricocheted off the fireplace before sinking into the floor. The sound joined the fear of seeing Mom on the floor with blood on her cheek.

"Now you know what I go through just to put food on the table," he said before turning away and going upstairs.

On Friday, May 11, 1979, Mother's Day weekend, was the last time. I could use the word "fight" to soften the image or make it sound like a domestic disagreement over the cost of groceries that got out of hand. There are ways to write that make the ugliness in human beings easier to understand. But if anyone ever reads this I want it understood that I am writing this to tell the truth from my heart so it will release the fear, anger, and hurt and let it fly away, dissipate, crumble to nothingness because as long as it is in my heart it has the power to damage, to recreate, to further its evil.

So I am pouring this story into the computer to remove it from me, but I do not tell it to hate my father, nor do I tell it to invite anyone else to hate him. I know he had goodness in him. I remember it from when he would call me to the swimming pool and motion me to sit beside him while he talked on the phone. For all the neighbors to see from their patios, he would stroke my hair, squeeze my shoulder, and then gently motion me away, setting me free to return to Mom or my room.

Sometimes when he came home after I had gone to bed he would waken me when he opened the door, but I would pretend to stay asleep. The smell of whiskey and restaurant food would settle on me when he came to my bedside, bend down, and rest his large open hand on my back. In the dark and silence of those few precious moments, I felt like both the giver and receiver in a story of ages.

He'd hand me a twenty dollar bill on Fridays and say, "A man's got to have money in his pockets." I was the talisman he liked to stroke once in a while to remind him of a goodness in himself he left behind. I believe he wanted me near at those moments to remind him of what he had been as a child, to touch his own deepest lost innocence. I do not know my father's story. Perhaps if I did, I would understand him better.

The last beating started as soon as he came home late on that May night. I was asleep and Mom was in bed reading. A rustle of sheets and blanket, a thud, and her short scream tore at the seams of the house before I heard my father slur, "Shut up." I lay on my back, staring at the ceiling, hearing the sounds I now knew well. Lying in bed I could feel the hits, I could see the beating, where the bruises would be on Mom, that were evidence of my father's growing danger. The growing emotional scars, mixed in my mind with affection, were leading me to a life I did not want.

I can't be sure what I was thinking at the time. Perhaps it was only emotion squeezing out caution, but I got up when it had gone on so long the sounds no longer surprised or sickened me. I walked to the open, beautiful French glass doors and took two steps inside. There I stood. A witness no longer objecting.

"Go Jake, go," Mom whispered when she saw me.

So I did.

Another minute or two of sound passed before I heard a thud in the hall. Then my mother's whimpering and finally the closing of the bathroom door. I was still awake when I heard her creep back to bed. Perhaps an hour passed. I got up and slowly turned the doorknob of my bedroom door. Lying in a large heap, covered only by the darkness of night, was my father. He protected the closed doors leading to his imprisoned woman.

I left my door open so there wouldn't be any noise closing it, and went back to bed. But there was no warmth in that bed. I gathered the bedspread around me and sat motionless. Time passed until my room was changing from black to dark grey. I got up again, and now helped by a lightening sky, easily found clothes to slip on.

I walked to my father's body. He was in his underwear, curled like a baby and snoring like a train whistle. Through the windows were the bedroom's shadows.

There was just enough room for a nine-year old boy to quietly step between my father and the door. Never had I been so careful about balance. Inch by inch I lowered the handle lever on one side and walked toward my mother's bedside. Before I reached her she quickly jerked her head, afraid of who it was. When she saw me she sat up.

Her face was bludgeoned. I could see the bruises growing on both cheeks. One eye was almost closed. Even nine year-olds know when there is no time to be sentimental. "Let's go."

She paused. Her eyes darted about, perhaps reflecting the dozen thoughts of fleeing and staying.

"We need to go."

She got up in a move that reminded me of a wind-up toy I had that would take three jerky steps and then fall down. She went to the closet, got a suitcase and began filling it. Last she walked to the dark bathroom, closed the door and dressed. I listened to my father's breath for any change and breathed through my mouth to be silent. Day was coming and I saw his clothes from yesterday thrown by a corner. Was my mother's blood on them? When Mom came out of the bathroom I stood and we turned toward the doors.

With the doors now open, it was easier to see a path around him. As we reached the top of the stairs, he moved, and we stopped until he was again settled in sleep. Mom pointed to the side of the staircase to indicate that we should avoid the sometimes creaking, tell-tale middle. In the kitchen she got the car keys from the basket by the fridge. Once in the carport, Mom whispered, "You push and I'll steer to the street."

The gold Cadillac Fleetwood was heavy, but a solid push in the middle by a kid on adrenalin has strength. The car rolled to the street, and she steered to go on the road. I opened the door and jumped in, but didn't close it, only held it, to prevent a noise. Mom and I looked at each other, my wide eyes with fear reflected back at me. We were sure if we woke the sleeping man he would fly out the window and catch us still.

The car rolled to a stop in the street. She turned the key and the large engine came awake. At the stop sign on the corner, I closed the passenger door and we drove away.

Chapter 6

"Come on, boy, come on."

Matthew Arnold

There's only so much horror anyone can stand at one time. A story can be retold, a feeling can be remembered, and then when it reaches a breaking point, the mind shuts down. That's when I turned the computer off that night and went to bed for the deepest sleep I'd had in weeks. Four hours later I drove to work. My mind wandered back to when I was a boy, but now it could pick up with good memories.

Mom has style. When she'd dressed that morning it wasn't whatever she could grab from the closet. Instinctively, she reached for a cream colored, tailored pantsuit from Lord and Taylor's in Chicago, a black silk blouse, and matching high heels. I wouldn't say I felt happy running from my father, or looking at my mother's ensemble, or seeing the horrified face on the receptionist when we walked in the emergency room door of the hospital in the next county. What I felt was a flood of release, a powerful peace that we had made it: like walking over a land mine and not losing a limb.

The receptionist immediately called for a doctor. Two hours later, with no questions asked about how it happened, we walked out and drove east into the late morning sun and the Pittsburgh Hilton's parking lot.

Memory had to step back when I pulled into the Great Party! parking lot. I needed to return to the demands of a small business and life as I was living it, and not how it was years ago. All day memories of that day in 1979 walked in and out of my head and I felt a strange mixture of sadness and relief. Committing my history to paper was giving me clarity and focus. That night I excused myself early and returned to my computer, sure about the time I now had to remember and record.

When Mom turned off the Cadillac in the Hilton parking lot she said, "I'm going to call Mother and Matt. We'll go there." While she was on the lobby pay phone, I stood six feet away, patrolling around her so no one would walk by and hear what she was saying.

When she stepped out of the booth, she turned to me. "After we eat here in the coffee shop, we're going to the airport to pick up our tickets to Seattle at the United Airlines desk. I could no longer read her expression behind the rhinestone-studded sunglasses.

I was always proud of my mother. She was the prettiest of all the moms who came to class. Her dark, thick hair tumbled to her shoulders, and her pale skin was like the china behind the glass in the dining room cabinet. Once she showed me a photo in Vogue of a woman in an evening gown. It looked like her.

Her model's grace gave her the majesty to own the plane with dignity that morning. Regal in her cream pantsuit and heels, she didn't falter as she walked down the airplane's aisle with a still growing bruise on her swollen cheek. The sunglasses hid her eyes, but darkening bruises couldn't be erased with make-up. Her lips were dabbed with a soft rose lipstick, but the gentle curve of one side of her face was ballooning like a slow torture in the circus macabre.

We arrived at the Seattle airport where Gran and Matt were to be waiting for us in the terminal. I didn't know who to look for. I was having a hard time remembering the details of pictures on a living room table and translating that to real people, but Mom had my hand and pulled me forward.

She lifted her other arm, "Mom."

I saw whose attention she was trying to get a second before they followed her familiar voice. The expression on the two older people's faces went from surprise to anger. Before we reached her Gran let out with a string of profanity right in the airport about who had done that to Mom's face. Matt quietly patted her shoulder saying, "There, there, Willie, she's here now."

The next morning was Easter, and Matt led me to the barn to show me around. "Come on boy, come on. You need to see where you live now," he said. We passed a ten foot by fifteen foot plot of turned dirt ready for summer vegetable planting before he led me to the chickens. "Well, will you look at that, new chicks. Looks like you've already got a responsibility here to look after these." A squirmy pile of moving slime and four beaks was only three feet from where I stood. "By tomorrow they'll be cute as Easter marshmallow chicks."

We walked to the barn where he showed me an old tractor, a riding mower, shovels, and a chain saw.

"It looks like we need another saw. I'll get one for you, and you can help me when the fence needs new ties."

I stared at the tall, skinny man wearing glasses I'd met only the day before. I thought he was crazy.

Gran and Matt were as new to me as the ocean they took me to see the next week. Life was suddenly indefinable, and at first felt otherworldly. I didn't understand easy conversation at the dinner table, or the big, spontaneous laughter from Gran who looked like a slightly heavier, older version of Mom; one who had muscle in her body and looked ready to leap to a fight that my mother could never have handled. I didn't understand the tall, thin man who happily enjoyed a single nightly Manhattan when he returned from work. His quiet, yet overseeing presence at the dinner table, or the way he would lean and just hug me baffled me, and I would step away from his arms. I didn't understand a barn in the backyard, chickens squawking in a pen, a tractor, a split-rail fence around the yard, or the country road where neighbors were half a block away.

At first all of it felt as fearful as when I looked into the deep end of the swimming pool in Steubenville. Everything was different from my old life. For the first weeks I insisted on sleeping with my mother. The clothes they bought me felt itchy and strange, the smooth wooden toy Matt carved and sanded for me looked made for a three-year-old, and I thought it was silly. My mother's easy laughter when she drank tea with Gran in the morning didn't sound like her.

It was only looking back years later that I realized that I had lived my first nine years in an underwater world holding my breath, and without knowing how I'd done it, surfaced and taken a frightening breath of a new life.

My dad called a few times, but I knew that only because I heard my grandmother yelling at him before banging down the phone. Other than that, everything that was my life in Steubenville was left behind.

Since only three weeks of school remained, no one bothered to make me go to school, and I was suddenly a kid on summer vacation who lived in a foreign land. Matt was the first to leave in the morning for his work as a computer technician with National Cash Register. Gran would leave about half an hour later for an office where she worked as a real estate agent.

During the first weeks I shadowed Mom as she moved around the house to watch television, or sit out in the sun on a patio ringed with blooming tulips. She seemed unsure of herself, more reluctant to leave the house than in Steubenville. I knew she was waiting for the bruises to completely fade, but there was a shadow in her eyes that needed time to heal from the inside, and she seemed as frail as the chicks.

More than once I overheard Gran and Mom sitting at the dining room table and Gran would say, "Men should never get under your skin like that," or "Get your strength back up, Mary, life has to be looked in the face for what it is." In the middle of the table would be a tall crystal vase filled with deep red roses. Matt had them sent to his wife from a florist every Friday afternoon. When I walked in to join them and sit at the table like I was part of the conversation, Gran would get the cards and we'd play hearts or Gin Rummy.

When the bruises were gone Mom started looking for work, and life smoothed into another rhythm. I watched a little television and read a few books when I was alone, but most of my memories are about the woman I began calling Gran, and the man I would later come to call Pap. At first I just watched, absorbing what was happening. Mom drifted in and out during the day depending on what she was doing and where she needed to be, but the evening started like a scheduled bell ring when Gran came in the door at four-thirty, changed into something "more comfortable," and returned to the kitchen. As she asked me how I spent my day and how the chicks where surviving my amateur care, she got glasses out and lined up bottles of whiskey, vermouth, and cherry juice to make Manhattans. One paper napkin would be placed on the counter where she then put two long-stemmed maraschino cherries to let the juice be absorbed. Next, she looked in the freezer or the cupboard to figure out what dinner would be. When she heard Pap's truck turning in the driveway, all focus turned to him.

Whatever she was doing would be interrupted to get ice out of the freezer to finish the Manhattans. There was always a hello embrace when he came in before he headed upstairs to wash up. The Manhattans would be put on a silver tray, with a last second addition of milk or juice for me, and Gran carried them into the living room and put them on the coffee table. Then she would sit in her recliner and motion for me to sit on the couch with my drink.

When Matt came down he would lift the glasses, present one to Gran, and then sit in his own chair eight feet away. I became aware of the lengthening days of summer sun coming through the light green sheer drapes behind the couch as I listened to their easy talk about what had happened that day. Matt talked about the computer that was installed and would be his responsibility to keep working well. "It's almost as big as this room," he indicated to the twelve by sixteen foot living room.

Gran talked about her clients and her co-realtor, the big-haired, "Good Time Gal," Klair, who was like a little sister. "She's having trouble, Matt. That no-good man of hers is better off gone, but those kids need some help."

"She's got reserve money in that Cadillac," Pap said.

"No she doesn't. She needs a car. I'm giving her my commission on the Denton sale."

"What?"

"I'm giving her my commission on the Denton sale next week."

"I heard that, but do you mean it?"

"Yes, those kids need it more than we do right now."

"Willie, your heart is bigger than that ocean out there," he indicated out the window and toward the Pacific.

He didn't have room to complain. I had already seen him drive his mower across the street to mow the acre-sized lawn of an old widow named Alice Telford, and together I would watch them tend animals for vacationing neighbors, pick up mail, invite people they thought were lonely to dinner, give Matt's wooden toys to children they barely knew, and leave a twenty dollar tip for the waitress at the Seabird Café who had fallen on hard times.

After the Manhattans, Gran would get up and I would follow her to help fix dinner. I avoided sitting alone in the same room as Matt. Men were tall, powerful, and full of bluster that exploded at odd, unpredictable times. I preferred having Gran teach me how to measure with teaspoons and cups, roll biscuits, place them on a baking sheet, and use a stiff, red-checkered mitt to get them out of the oven.

On a Saturday in early June, Mom was on the patio reading a magazine when I wandered around the barn to check on the chicks. All of them ate on their own, but since I'd been charged with caring for them I offered them seed from my hand so I could get close enough to touch. As their down turned to feathers it seemed a miracle.

I was walking by the wood shop when Matt yelled, "Here boy, you can finish this up." He handed me the broom and returned to the eight-foot door he was sanding. "I wonder if that woman will ever have enough space to keep things."

I'd heard my dad's voice when he complained about what Mom wanted, and I knew Matt wasn't complaining at all. He was making a door for a broom closet to be tucked in a corner of the kitchen. Since he made all the cabinets in the kitchen, it would be as sturdy and perfectly fitting as the others. The solid brass knobs were ordered from back east since, according to Gran, it was "impossible to find good quality in this back country."

Over dinner that week, Gran and Matt decided I needed a bedroom of my own. On Saturday, Matt called me in to lay down newspaper in a basement room off the family room before he painted it yellow, but I hadn't asked why Gran made me haul boxes of ribbon, glue, staplers, oil paints, brushes, and canvas from a room upstairs. "You can use my craft room. A bed is being delivered this week and we'll find you a desk." The half dozen shirts and two pairs of pants I had gotten since leaving everything behind were taken to the room that night and put in the closet. Gran left a chest for me she had used to store ribbons, threads, and fabric, as well as a strange hot-pink circular rug with the longest shag I'd ever seen. I emptied the closet of three boxes of rocks she had collected. "Matt's putting in shelves to put those on after he finishes the broom closet." She began telling me about how she liked to polish them.

A few days later I was again out checking on the chicks. They weren't quite as interesting to me anymore, but having them nibble from my hand was enjoyable, and I liked touching their changing feathers. The one standing on the end stumbled, fell, and looked too dizzy to stand up on its own. When it couldn't get up, the others scurried off, leaving it abandoned. That's life. Even Frank Sinatra sang about it on Gran's record. It must be the same for chickens.

"Boy, come here, I've got a job for you." Matt was leaning out his work shop door. "Here, hold that end while I measure." He lifted a two by four and I took the end.

"The tulips were pretty," I stuttered uncertainly. He looked at me through his safety glasses, handed me a pair and looked down again. The tulip petals had been falling off for over a week. "I liked the red color. Like the flag. The American flag. Father's Day . . . I don't know . . . He might want a present. The red tulips are the prettiest. Across the street I saw Mrs. Telford has yellow ones, but they aren't as pretty." My talk had turned into chatter, and I stopped to watch Matt saw the wood where he'd measured.

"This afternoon I need your help cutting the aspens that fell last winter." He blew the dust off the wood. "The fence has a couple of weak spots."

He'd kept his word. I now had my own chain saw hanging by his in the barn with a pair of safety glasses.

"Here boy, you do this one." That afternoon he stepped to the side after we'd put a fallen aspen on sawhorses and he pointed to the end, about two feet down from where the top branch was lifeless. "Now remember what I told you."

Hoisting the saw in front of me, I held it with my gloved hands, pushed the lever with my thumb, settled my weight with the vibrating machine, and slowly cut through the four inch pale tree. When the top fell I released the lever and looked at Matt. He pointed to the middle point of the tree between two sawhorses and I then cut through six inches.

We worked for an hour, maybe two, taking turns with both of us hoisting the fallen trees, me cutting the top trunk, Matt cutting the rest. After six trees made a pile, it was decided we were finished for the day and we headed to the shower.

I was the second one to come downstairs and into the kitchen in my clean shirt and pants. Matt and Gran were having coffee. "Willie, the boy and I have an errand to do. We're going to Padgett's, so tell Mary we won't be long." I hadn't any idea where we were going or why, and I wasn't sure I wanted to go alone with him. I'd never been alone with him.

His big red truck was rumbling down the long road into town and toward Padgett's Pharmacy when he said, "What do you buy for Father's Day?"

I cleared my throat. "Mom and I would get him a shirt and tie from Lord and Taylor's. Once we had his initials embroidered on the cuff. Or a golf shirt. He didn't golf though."

"Padgett's won't have all that."

"Matt, honey, what brings you in today?" A woman walked toward us almost as soon as we walked in the door, "Oh, you have a new friend. Howdy there, my name's Margie." We shook hands.

"Hi, Margie, this is Jake, he's Willie's grandson, and he needs a Father's Day gift."

"Oh, that is coming up. A lot of people have been coming in for that. Got anything in mind, honey?"

"No."

"What have you got, Margie?"

"Around here the most popular things are the fishing poles and flies. We've been selling a lot of fishing vests this year. Your dad into that?"

"No."

"Well, maybe then binoculars. Got a new Kodak camera people seem to like. A lot of men are getting a new toolbox we've got in the back. It could take a ride with you, Matt, in the back of that Ford of yours, and not take a dent with that bumpy ride of yours. When are you going to get an automatic? See anything, Jake?"

I shook my head.

"I think the boy's dad will manage with a half decent cologne."

"Okay! Now we're talking," said Margie as she turned to lead the way. Matt paid for the bottle of British Sterling and saved me from having to explain it. He carried in the Padgett's sack and set it on the dining room table where Mom and Gran were seated with a box of Gran's rock collection in front of them.

"The boy needs this mailed for Father's Day. I'll wrap it tonight."

Gran polished rocks, made baby blankets, cooked all meals, cleaned the whole house, but she couldn't wrap a present past the standards of a first grader. Matt's offer saved Mom and me from doing it and was one more gift to me while he watched me accustom myself to a new life and slowly learn that not all men were like my father.

The next morning Mom was upstairs getting dressed and Gran and I were finishing our pancakes when Matt came in. "One of the chicks is sick. Vomiting. It looks like a virus from what I've seen before."

"I hope it's not that virus I heard the Bartons had in their coop. It could contaminate them all."

"That's why the chick's got to go. Jake, they're your

animals. You need to kill it. I'll get the hatchet."

Gran stood up, "Matt, I don't think . . ."

"Willie, it's part of farming. A responsibility of owning animals."

Gran's brows furrowed, and she looked at me with a question in her eyes. I didn't move.

"Come on, boy, I'll meet you out there."

The screen door slammed and I still didn't move. The grey shadows of my last morning in my bedroom fell around the kitchen. I felt my father's breathing in the hall. I saw the blood on my mother's face and its drying, cracked riverbed down her neck when I woke her. Slowly I rose, but my steps out of kitchen were the memory of that morning. Determination without any thought. Just something that needed to be done. Gran watched me and followed. When we got to the chicks, closer to chickens now, I saw the sick one laying on its side. It's head was in a greenish, stinky vomit.

"You hold the hatchet like this, Jake."

I saw the hatchet raised in Matt's hand, but I didn't move. I saw Mom on the floor, the blood was red, streaming from her ear, through her curls and down her neck while Dad stood over her.

"No, Matt. I'll not have him do this. He wasn't brought up on a farm. He grew up with a weak monster. No, Matt," and she took my upper arm and pulled me back to the kitchen.

With the bruises gone, Mom was out looking for

work. She wasn't sure she could do anything. It had been several years since she was employed and her spirit was torn.

"You be strong, Mary, there's no room for weak people in this world. You have to move on," Gran said to her over dinner.

"She'll be working in no time," Matt said. "She's too pretty not to hire, isn't she Jake?"

She sure was, and as the summer went on her cheeks were beginning to glow like the pink roses in Gran's front yard. Her hair bounced in lively curls a hairdresser told her "had only been waiting to be let loose like in a Botticelli painting." Before the middle of August she was working as a travel agent for an airline during the day and at night as a bank check coder. Gran started looking for a place for Mom and me to live before the school year started.

The night before we were to move into an apartment where I would begin fifth grade, Pap knocked on my bedroom door.

"Come in, Pap." It was already August. I was comfortable in this bedroom and wasn't sure I wanted to move. Mom was my mom, but I felt stirrings I didn't understand for this older couple that three months earlier I'd only known from photos and a few phone conversations. Now I knew how to mix a Manhattan, talk about the day, make biscuits for dinner, cut timber, measure twice before sawing a two by four, and how to accept a dozen red roses at the door on Friday before giving the delivery boy a tip. I knew how to leave the women and go with Pap on Saturday mornings to the Kingston Ferry Dock to buy fresh crab for dinner.

"Jake, I want to say something."

I watched him where he sat on my bed.

"You know how your grandma is."

"Yes," I said, though I didn't know what he meant.

"She does all the excitement around this house. I do background acts." We looked at each other, "First, I want you to know that this will always be your bedroom. You've got a place here."

"Oh."

"She sent me in to say this. But I mean it, too. Men don't hurt women, and they don't have to kill animals to be men."

I nodded. He got up and walked over to hug me, but I stepped back and he stopped.

"You come back on weekends when you're not in school. We can still go to the wharf and the Seabird Café for lunch. I need help with the fence."

After he left I put back the pillow I had packed to take. It could stay and be my pillow here.

Chapter 7

"I have four rules."

Alwida Arnold

Writing at night was leaving me physically tired but mentally excited that I was capturing something. I couldn't say exactly what I was capturing, only that it felt necessary, exhilarating, and a little frightening.

Over the next week I wrote about the magic I remembered of that summer with my grandparents. I made notes during my Great Party! work days between working on a stack of invoices for an event, or calculating payroll. Odd moments of memory would return like when Pap and I would be sent to the Kingston Ferry Docks to buy fresh crab so Gran could make her crab casserole for dinner. On the way, he'd stop in a parking lot and teach me how to drive his stick-shift Datsun King Cab.

"A man's not worth his own weight if he can't drive stick," he'd say as we lurched along. Then he showed me how to drive the tractor, hold the sander, cut wood, and mend a fence.

After Mom and I moved into the apartment, I'd call Gran and ask if I could spend the weekend with them whenever Mom had to work. Gran never said no, so off I would go to follow my grandparents in whatever they were doing, just to be around them and feel the safety of walking over the pink shag rug and sleeping on the pillow I had left behind. I persuaded them to order pizza which I loved but, years later, I learned Pap grudgingly tolerated for me what he thought was slop. His preference was roasted duck from their brood. Gran taught me to make the barbecue sauce, how to baste, turn it, and arrange it on her china platter; perhaps all the while inadvertently laying the foundation for the work I am in today.

On a Thursday, which was slowly trudging along, I was talking with a food sales rep when I saw that Ann was calling me on the phone. I let it go to voice mail and finished the meeting about Great Party's readiness to move to a new price level in buying.

It was mid afternoon before I got around to listening to her voice mail. "Jake, I've decided you're right. It's time Liz came to see you. She needs a little dad time, so why don't you call this evening after seven and ask her to come spend spring break with you. That's it, bye." Astounding, I thought, but I wasn't going to argue this opportunity. Whatever her real reason, it sounded like it could work to my favor. I'd make sure to call.

Then there was the Logan problem. Though I'd been told weeks ago he was going by the house at odd times during the day, I avoided asking about him, preferring to remain as far away as possible from the appearance of favoritism or some sort of strange employer/employee relationship. There was no telling what could backfire. I avoided any conversation with him and only nodded from time to time to Melissa and Todd.

I was still at Great Party! when it would have been a few minutes after seven in Missouri. The office would be quiet until the truck came back around nine after a golden wedding anniversary. How did people stay married like that? I tried not to think further. Another partner in my life at this time would only complicate things. I dialed.

"Hi, Dad."

"Hi, Liz, what's up in crazy, lazy Kansas City . . . Kansas City here I come?"

"Oh, Dad, please don't sing that song."

"Well, then tell me what you're doing."

"Homework."

"Liz, come see us. When's your spring break? You could visit with Gran. She doesn't have a lot of time left and she'd love to see you."

She sighed a fourteen-year-old's sigh, "I guess I could. But you'd have to take me to Park City."

"For shopping and dinner. No problem."

"Okay, then." After that all we talked about was what time and days I should buy the plane tickets for.

Over the next two weeks whenever I walked in a room

where Mom and Gran were, they would be talking about Liz's visit. I was as excited as they were, but I had found out the real reason Ann had prodded Liz to come. She wanted her to find the missing box. Fine, I thought. Have at it, but we weren't going to spend too much precious time looking for something that had already been looked for three times.

The plan I had pledged to follow was to pick Liz up from the airport and whisk her back to the house for a home-cooked dinner, something Gran and Mom imagined she had not experienced for some time.

Luckily, the early Wednesday evening flight she came in on was on time, so plans and temperaments remained stable. There was plenty to catch up on and we spent a great deal of time trying to figure out whose genes were responsible for her burst of three inches of growth since we had last seen her, and just where in the family line that curly, honey brown hair came from. We all wanted credit and Ann's side was not considered at all. Another child might have been overwhelmed by the scrutiny, but I was surprised Liz lost her telephone voice attitude and temporarily returned to the freshness and pleasure she showed in younger years when she spent time with her grandmothers.

It was near frightening to look at Liz. I hadn't seen her for six months and during that time her transformation was achingly beautiful. She was changing from the straight lines of girlhood to the curves of a young woman. It was all I could do not to throw a blanket around her to keep the world from seeing. How could I let this treasure, this child growing up, ever meet the dangers of the world without me around?

The next two days were a whir of activity. I went in to the office early in the mornings and left by noon to finish the work day via telephone. The burden and extra work fell on Tim and Chef Don's shoulders but they could handle it. I told Mom that Liz had been instructed to find that stupid box, so while I was at the office, she was to help Liz look.

"What's in the box?" Mom asked

"I don't know. Maybe piles of money"

"How are we supposed to know which box it is?"

"On the top is written, 'Stay out. This means you. Ann's box.'"

"Brilliant. She was always so brilliant."

Friday I'd reserved Liz to be mine alone. I picked her up at two and we headed to Park City to spend the rest of the day and the night. It was our father-daughter treat and I hoped to make it memorable. There was still time before she left on Sunday, but I already hurt thinking of saying goodbye.

We checked into the stately Deer Valley Lodge for the night, but Liz wanted to go into town and shop before dinner to get away from this "stuffy" place. "There's only women in white fur hats with Botox-ed foreheads here, Dad." She was wrong, but I remembered the call to more action when I was fourteen, too.

Few creatures in this world seem happier than a shopping female with a man who promises unlimited buying power. We went from shop to shop all up and down old Main Street. We shopped for boots, earrings (newly pierced a month previous I learned), the oddest assortment of clothes I had seen in a long time, and, of course, there was a nostalgic stroll through several stuffed animal sections. She held a cuddly rhinoceros with both arms, only very reluctantly putting it down.

"Are you sure you don't want the rhino, Liz?"

She turned sharply, taking one more step from childhood, "I'm sure, Dad."

Three packages and several hundred dollars later, she was the one who suggested dinner, "I want to go to Riverhorse."

The popular restaurant was beginning to fill, but we slipped in early enough that we didn't have to wait. Luckily, we got a table toward an end that didn't get the full din of voices and clattering plates and glasses echoing between tintype ceiling, wood floors, and metal tables.

"Great choice, Liz. I haven't eaten here since you and I last did, two years ago."

Her nod let me know she remembered.

There was a busy few minutes while we read the menu, met our waiter, and tried to decide between the scallops with Thai noodles and papaya, sweet potato ravioli in pesto, or the lamb shank with oregano pomegranate mint sauce. I settled on the lamb and Liz chose the noodles, but would only order them as long as I promised to eat the scallops.

"You need to develop a taste for seafood, Liz."

"Ick. Not in Kansas City I don't."

"Then at least get Gran's barbecue sauce recipe before you go. It'll put you on the map in Kansas City."

"Yeah."

I needed to ease my way into approaching this half-child, half-woman. "Did I ever tell you about the dinners Gran would make when I stayed with them?"

"Yes."

"She'd start in the afternoon on a Saturday setting the table and planning what we were going to have. With duck it was usually rice, but sometimes potatoes and some vegetable. Sometimes there would be a pineapple and coconut salad or Caesar."

"And you would help her."

"Even with making the Manhattans she and Pap had."

"In the morning it was always either pancakes or waffles. That's what Pap loved," she echoed from past re-tellings.

"You like those, too."

"No. They'll make you fat."

"You shouldn't stop eating the foods you love."

"Did you like school, Dad?"

Her abrupt left turn change in subject surprised me.

"I changed schools a lot."

"But did you like it?"

How does a parent encourage a child to love school when he hated it? "I managed. How are you enjoying your new school?"

She shrugged her shoulders.

"I know, Liz. It's tough. It's not at all easy to change schools. Kids can be hard to meet."

"They're not hard to meet. I know all their names."

"That's a good start."

"Sometimes I wish I were back here."

"I wish you were, too."

"Mom doesn't ever want to come back to Utah."

"You are always welcome here, Liz. This is your home. You will always be welcome with me."

"What was school like for you, Dad, when you moved to Washington?"

"It was a challenge. Not one I always handled very well. I was only nine and not very good at making friends. I felt awkward. I also had come from a long ways away. Even the way the kids walked seemed different in Ohio than Washington."

"The girls wear their hair different."

"Still, underneath it all, don't you think the kids are the same here and there?"

"Maybe. I don't know. How did you make friends there? Who was your best friend?"

"I made a friend named Harden. It was Harden Pomeroy, and I think he took pity on me when I turned up at school looking too sexy for my shirt." Might as well throw in a little humor with a song lyric.

Liz looked up and smiled with the betwixt beauty of innocence and promise of a fourteen-year-old. How, I thought, do I get through to this girl and send her home with something to protect her?

"What was he like?"

"Well, he wore great acid-washed jeans. He liked to snap his head so his hair would move back on his shoulder. He thought that was really cool to catch girls. Not that I remember that it ever did. We were still just boys. Ten years old."

"What would you do?"

"We'd go to movies. That was when Indiana Jones first came out. Mostly we just hung around like kids do. When your grandma and I moved there I spent a lot of time at Gran and Pap's. They were my refuge."

"What about when you were my age?"

"Well, let's see, by then Harden had moved away. I think his dad got a new job out of state, and I was going to another new school because my mother was married again."

By the time we finished dessert, I'd repeated what she'd already heard at family gossip sessions. Mom's husband number two never beat her, but he had his own faults. While they dated he was Mr. Nice Guy who brought flowers and candy for Mom and cassette tapes of Pat Benetar, Foreigner and an REO Speedwagon for me. Once he even took me fishing out in the bay, and I did catch my one and only fish, a halibut.

Full of hope and sure she was giving me a good man to follow, Mom married Mr. Chameleon who, once he felt enthroned as head of a household, became a dictator. Husband number two, Ron Thomas, insisted on a side part in my hair that might have been popular in World War II, plain-colored shirts tucked in slacks, and loafers, definitely not popular at the time. With Harden gone and in another new school, my enforced boarding school clothes only drove a wedge between me and any hope of finding friends and fitting in at school.

While we drove back to Deer Valley Lodge I tried to squeeze in what I really wanted to get through to her. "Remember, Liz, these last few years of school before college are only a very few years of your life, but the decisions you make will make a difference for as long as you live."

She was looking out the window at the people walking between bars and restaurants.

"You can always come back here, Liz. You have family that will always be here for you, no matter what happens."

The next morning we had brunch at the Lodge before heading over to the Kimball Art Center where there was a show of wood carvings and sculptures named "Western Land Art."

"Why do you want to see this, Dad?"

"Maybe Gran could use some new ideas for her wood carvings." I think it was nostalgia that made me stop because Gran had given it up years ago.

Only half a dozen people were wandering through the rooms while looking at strangely shaped driftwood, tree trunks, rock arrangements, and bronze sculptures. Artists had inserted personality into driftwood and broken tree branches. Rock arrangements secured by wire took on strangely human forms.

"Gran hasn't worked on wood for a long time has she, Dad?"

"No, but I thought a new idea may inspire her."

"There's a wood shop class at school."

"Oh?"

"Mom wants me to take ceramics."

"What do you want to take?"

"I don't know." We wandered through the exhibit making a few comments about the works, but what I remember was the easiness that had returned between Liz and me. She mentioned the names of a few friends and told me a little about them. We talked about a good pizza place they'd found, and she laughed about a date Ann had who brought along his Great Dane, Theo. As long as I could keep that comfortable feeling between Liz and me, everything else between Ann and me would be forced to settle.

When we got home I made a few calls to the office to check on things for the three small events we had that Saturday evening, and Mom and Liz gave a last effort to look for Ann's box, but when it didn't show up no one tried again. By the end of the day, Liz and I settled around the kitchen table to watch Gran and Mom fix dinner.

"Dad thought your driftwood pieces should have been in the show at the Kimball Art Center, Gran."

"Oh, yes? Then they should have."

"Especially your piece on the wall there, the one that you call But Beautiful," I said.

"Why is it named that, Gran?"

"Oh, honey, that's from an old Frank Sinatra song, But Beautiful.

"Tell Liz when you first heard that song, Mother."

Gran stopped helping Mom in the kitchen and turned, leaned on her walker, and softly said, "'Love is funny or it's sad, Or it's quiet or it's mad, It's a good thing or it's bad, But beautiful.' That song meant so much to me when I first heard it. It was in Road to Rio, and I was in New York all by myself. I was going to school, but I felt so lonely. The jerk Clive had left me, and I had left my baby with my mother. It was the loneliest time of my life in that big city of millions of people."

"I was fine, Mom."

"I knew you were, Mary," her voice was a bit strident and defensive. "But I also knew moms shouldn't leave their babies no matter the circumstances. But I'd gotten myself into a mess with a no good man, and I needed to damn well get out of it."

"And you did."

"Yes, I did. I've got to sit down. Mary, you're on your own for dinner. Jake or Liz can help." Both Liz and I jumped up to help her to a chair. "When I got back to Pennsylvania it wasn't any better, I'll tell you that. It took years. Years!"

"But you did it, Mother. You found Matt."

"Eventually, but let me tell you," and she looked directly into Liz's eyes, "you don't ever want to be where I was. I came home and my baby, my daughter right here this kitchen, didn't even know me. She'd completely forgotten all about her mama."

"But that didn't last long."

"No, no, but it was a hurt for a long time. You were close to your grandma. Closer to her than I'd ever been. You two had a bond."

"Gran went to work for Van Heusen Shirts." Mom said, changing the subject.

"Yes, that was my first job in accounting. No one, and I mean no one, was fun in that office. Laughter just didn't happen in that airless fortress. So as soon as I could, I looked for other work."

"But you were starting to earn good money."

"I earned a little money and I was tough with it. I made a nickel scream for its life."

"You bought Cousin Lorine's wedding dress."

"She was almost as stupid and poor as I had been, but I wanted her to have good memories, so I bought it. Someone should start with dreams coming true. I want you to do that, Liz."

The pork tenderloin with a coriander rub, roast potatoes, asparagus, Caesar salad, and warm rolls were ready so we took a break to bring it all to the table. After a toast to a wonderful weekend and family, Gran continued.

"Your Grandma Mary wasn't any smarter with Jake's dad, but she has been able to make peace with it. She does know the end of the story and that matters. Isn't that right, Mary?"

"Yes, Liz. There will be some things you won't be able to control in life, but you can control your reaction," Mom said.

Gran picked up, "You've heard how that monster beat your grandma and scared your poor daddy when he was a boy."

Liz nodded, "Yes."

"So what does your Grandma Mary do? Hate him? Never speak to him again? That's what he deserves," Gran continued, "but instead she sends monster Pete dozens of Christmas cookies. Can you believe it?"

"You send him cookies, Grandma?"

"Liz, it's one of the things life just forces into you. You can either hate the meanness that is done to you with equal meanness, or you can put it aside and look at it from a different view. If you keep the meanness, you can feel it grow inside of you like a cancer. You can feel it grow in your heart and move good feelings aside. It took years, but when I saw Jake was better, and I was better, I looked at the life of that man, looked at where he is now, and I thought, 'He has nothing. No one to live with who loves him. No lasting friends.' He's ill now. Dying I hear. He threw away his best chance at happiness when he was cruel to Jake and me. He is to be pitied. So I send him cookies at Christmas and his birthday to show him and remind myself that there are better ways to think and live."

"And Gran, you did find Matt."

"Yes, I finally did. A friend told me about a job in a nightclub in Steubenville that had the best live music in three states. It was also time for Mary and me to be on our own. I needed my daughter to myself, and the only way to make that happen was to leave Bakerton."

I knew the story well enough to start it. "And what a nightclub! Dean Martin sang there before he got famous. Steubenville was his hometown."

"He was the one who introduced me to Matt," Gran said while nodding.

Liz had heard that story, but we all enjoyed hearing it again.

"The thing is, Liz, this time I'd learned. Oh, how I'd learned. I was so crazy about Matt I would have fallen off Mt. Everest for him, but when he proposed I stood up from the kiss he was giving me, and I left him holding the ring in the box and I said, 'Matt, I will only marry you if you follow my four rules.' His chin dropped and I said, 'The four rules are: Don't play around on me. Don't lie to me. Don't ever publicly embarrass me. And if you ever lay a mean hand on me or my daughter, I'll kill you where you stand.'"

When Liz and I were ready to leave for the airport the next day, Gran and Mom gave Liz especially hard hugs. Gran held her close. "Now don't you forget where you come from, Elizabeth Buchanan. There's strong woman blood in you. You're a part of us and we will always, *always* welcome you home."

Chapter 8

"There isn't a no to me."

Pete Buchanan

The end of March was one long stretch of cold rain that would turn to the long drippy mush of coming spring. Work took most of my time. If I wasn't making sales calls, I was working on bids or helping in the back for that day's events. My time home was usually from ten at night until six or seven in the morning when I'd catch up on Mom's reports of Gran's doctor visits. There still wasn't any time for a love life, and no one to have one with anyway.

When Mom and I left Dad in the early morning hours of May when I was nine, I learned life can change in an instant. But for now, my life was filled with work and spending as much time as possible helping Mom with Gran, as well as spending real time with Gran, herself. Deep down I also knew I needed this private space of time in my life to heal from the divorce. I didn't want to blindly walk into another situation where I was repeating my mistakes. I knew my love life needed this time off, though convincing Eric of that was difficult.

Eric and I were walking from the court after finishing a game of racquetball, and I was trying to end a conversation about what he thought I needed in a woman, when my phone rang.

"Hi, Mom."

"Jake, I need you to go pick up Gran and take her to her doctor appointment. I'm stuck here in the parking lot at Costco with a flat tire and the AAA truck isn't going to be here in time. I think I ran over a nail in a construction zone."

"Okay, sure. I can do that. Good luck with the tire."

I turned off the phone and turned to Eric who was dripping with sweat from the game I gave him. "Your standard lecture number six-zero-four will have to wait. I've got to take Gran to a doctor appointment.

"I'll pick up where I left off tomorrow," he said. I knew he meant well and only wanted to be a cheerleader.

At home, the sound of the car in the driveway would have been expected with Mom's return, and so would have the opening of the back door. They were still chatting when I walked into the living room.

"Gran, I'm here to take you to the doctor appointment. Mom had a flat tire."

"Hello, Mr. Buchanan, I'll be going now," Logan jumped up from the couch where he'd been turned to directly face Gran in her chair.

"Hi, Jake. So it's time for another damn doctor. They keep sprouting in my life like wild asparagus. Bye Logan. Now you take care of yourself, boy."

"Bye, Ms. Alwida," he had reached the door and slipped out.

"You could at least be civil with the boy. He didn't do anything wrong," Gran said.

"It's not good that employees are in this house."

"Well, I can't exactly meet him in a bar or I would. Go get my purse, Jeeves. I'll wait here." Gran's sarcasm was her power and nobody questioned it.

Her appointment was the doctor's last one of the day so the wait was almost half an hour, though we were the only ones in the room. At first we didn't talk because she was torturing me for my treatment of Logan.

"Doctor offices always make me feel so sad," she said.

"Why's that?" I continued looking at my Sports Illustrated.

"I remember holding Matt's hand when he went to doctors. Time and again we went for him, and it never seemed to do any good."

"He was sick a long time."

"All that pain he suffered, and he still had my roses sent every Friday. He still remembered every birthday, every anniversary, every Valentine's."

On the way home we were in commuter traffic inching along when it began to snow a mushy, March storm. "Jake, you're living through a difficult time now."

I didn't answer.

"But you need to remember. People don't always appreciate the good if they've never had the bad. This thing you went through with Ann was ugly. But you got Liz from it. At my age you look through a longer lens. What I went through with Clive Stewart was ugly. But I got your mother from it. I didn't appreciate that at the time. I was nineteen and scared, and sometimes I couldn't tell if I loved that baby or if I was angry at it for being born."

"I can understand."

"But time went on and things changed. Your mother, my baby, is a good, *good* woman, and she always deserved more than I could give her."

"You did fine by her, Gran."

"Things will change for you too, Jacob."

Gran's reminisces were becoming more frequent. Most of what she talked about I'd heard through the years, but it was always told with her biting humor edged with sarcasm. Now it seemed she was viewing her memories through a softer light of gratitude and peace.

"Be kind when you can to Logan. He needs it and he looks up to you."

I gave her a withering look, which ignited her snappy voice. "Listen, the poor boy's grandma, the only one he knew, died when he was ten and his dad died two years ago. Give him a break."

That night after Gran and Mom went to bed, I again went to the computer. I checked on the company emails, but my thoughts were far away. Nothing was urgent, so I opened a new file and typed a few lines.

Time heals all wounds.

Be kind.

Be grateful.

Give breaks.

Words from Gran.

Louise Bates popped into my mind. Mom didn't make the same mistake twice in her choice for a second husband. Ron Thomas's method of control wasn't beatings. He didn't ever lay a hand on Mom, or on me. He was around the house a lot more often and on weekends he was more like Pap than my father in how he spent time mowing the lawn, fixing leaky faucets, and cleaning his prized barbecue.

But he was a man of order and discipline. Nickels needed to flip on made beds. Fresh apples needed to be arranged in perfect symmetry in the white bowl on the kitchen counter. As I'd told Liz, his uniform for me to wear to school was pressed slacks, and a plain color shirt tucked in with a leather belt showing. Shoes were brown and my hair was to be combed and smooth in the fashion he had worn to school. That same outfit was to be seen at the dinner table where he presided.

A new father. Another new school. An undeveloped, deeply frightened spirit. No social skills with peers. That was my resume to begin middle school. It got me exactly what would be expected—an attitude of belligerence, rebellion away from home, and a cowed, angry, but quiet attitude at home.

The few friends I made were outsiders like me who drifted toward dangerous parties and behavior. Ernie was an okay-looking kid who could get the girls to talk to him when he recited poetry, but he was otherwise forgettable and most kids ignored him. Carson was another transplant like me who came from Albuquerque, but his family moved every six months when a landlord finally demanded current rent payments. We called ourselves the Three Musketeers to bolster our shredded dignity at school where the kids ignored us, though they did tell Ernie where the parties were scheduled when he begged, and some of them would talk to us at those.

Everyone knows teenagers go to parties on weekends, come home late, and then sleep until noon. I was young and my body handled it, or so I thought, and I imagined it didn't show at home. Away from home, between classes, after school, and most weekends, I spent my time with Ernie and Carson, who were as wasted and lost as me.

The only positive, independent effort I made during this time was joining the school yearbook staff. But even with the study types, I felt worthless or comical in my clothes. On top of that, my ability to make the kind of small talk they liked was non-existent, because I didn't understand what they liked at all.

There isn't a lot I like to tell and less I want to remember about that time. My choices weren't good though they were innocent, and in the beginning only experimental and on weekends. At home I followed the rules of behavior and learned to deal with the dismissive looks I got from kids over my brown leather shoes and pressed shirts. What I remember most is walking alone through the halls with no one to say hi to or give a high five. I felt ugly, unloved, and utterly alone.

I didn't want to spend time with my grandparents anymore. I'd grown up, and they were childhood toys and illusions that needed to be set aside. I thought of them from time to time, but it was with a nostalgia a fourteen-year-old can't indulge for fear of jeopardizing budding manhood. Eventually Mom and Ron suspected what was going on. The first time the school called because I'd missed class I was only told to cut it out. But then Mom smelled the oversweet alcohol of the night before in my bedroom when she went in to change my sheets. One night she was watching television in the dark when I came home. Her eyes widened and grew more alarmed as she watched me stumble through the room and toward the hall, but she didn't say anything. The next morning, instead of calling my name from the door to wake me, she came inside and sat on my bed.

"Jake, wake up."

I didn't move until she said it again and louder. Then I only looked at her.

"Jake, you look terrible. Don't drink. That's not good, especially in excess. It's dangerous and you could hurt yourself."

I felt relieved she had found me out, but I reacted angrily by pulling covers over my head and yelling at her. "Get out of my room. Don't I get any privacy?"

She nagged me over the next month, but she didn't have the ability to follow me around or enforce anything anymore. She was still holding down two jobs, and Ron required a lot of attention when he was home. They were also in the middle of looking for a home on Whidbey (pronounced "Would-be") Island, a place where they figured they could get a fresh start and a bigger house than where we were living.

They weren't considering my life at all. Or at least that's how I saw it. Who did they think they were, moving me again to a new school full of new people? Didn't they know how hard it was for a person like me to make friends? I wasn't a football hero, a basketball star, or even a kid who had a personality people liked. I was shut out from the people I wanted to know at school, and now I was shut out from my mother's life. On top of all that, Ron was making us move to a puny, godforsaken island in the middle of nowhere. I'd be a prisoner.

Ron finally noticed me when it became public that his control over a teenager wasn't working. On a late September Saturday night, Ernie, Carson, and I went to a party we'd heard about at Lighthouse Park. Ernie was the driver, and on the way home he bumped the car in front of us at a red light as we drove through town. Rather than deal with crazy teenagers, the couple called the police. Today they probably throw kids in detention facilities, but back then they called home and I was busted.

Mom arrived at the scene with wild eyes, then ran over to hug me and make sure I was all right. Ron was beside her, burning with an anger so deep he could barely talk to the policeman. On the way to the car he didn't talk to either Mom or me and his anger seemed like ice.

At home our argument lasted for over an hour, only breaking up when I yelled from out of nowhere, "I want to go live with my father."

Mom looked like she'd been hit with a bullet, but Ron sneered, "We'll see what we can do about that."

Within a month I was on a plane headed back to Ohio. It had been five years since I'd seen my dad though we'd kept in touch. It was rare, but I had talked with him on the phone, and he'd sent a photo of him and his new wife, Roxanne, when they were married a couple of years earlier. He was still in the same house and said I could have my old room back. Roxanne would take her fur coat and a few extra clothing items she had out of there to make room for me.

The reunion was awkward, but surprisingly sincere. Dad gave me a real smile when he first saw me walk in the airport terminal, and Roxanne's eyes finally settled on me when she realized who I was. Dad's back slaps felt comfortable and welcome. He'd gained a few pounds, but he looked more muscular and his shirts looked more expensive.

"Nice to meet you, Jake." Roxanne was a stiff Kewpie doll who looked like a prize given out on midways for hitting five baskets in a row. She wore a soft pink and yellow silk scarf around her neck, and smelled like bourbon and a tropical flower perfume.

The bedroom hadn't been changed, and when I went to bed that night I realized that the sheets hadn't been either. Other parts of the house had changed. There was new living room furniture, kitchen cabinets, and a whole new set of bedroom furniture in my dad, and now Roxanne's, room. Outside my bedroom, the only furniture that still remained from when I lived there was the dining room table. Later I learned it was only there because my father had forgotten about it, and I don't think Roxanne had ever even walked through the dining room.

Instead of the stiff dinner conversations from when Mom and I lived there, meals now were all take-out to be eaten in front of the television in the family room, at the kitchen counter, or outside by the pool on whatever plate anyone happened to pull from the cupboard. The backyard still felt like a park without any fences. The lack of fences and wide open spaces meant eyes could see far and ears could listen.

The neighbors hadn't changed either. I could still see the Jarsevick's greenhouse at the end of the block where I had sometimes played, and I saw the same lace curtains on Louise Bates's kitchen window. She and her husband, Art, lived next door. Louise was a petite Italian Catholic lady who

I was already taller than when Mom and I had left four years earlier. She would often rush out her door and wave me over so she could give Mom and me a paper plate stacked with chewy Italian pignolli or crispy aniseed cookies.

The first Saturday I was there Louise walked across her backyard to where I was eating ice cream while dad read the newspaper.

"Come to mass with me this Sunday, Jake," she said. We'll go to dinner after."

Years before she'd taken me to mass a couple of times, and though I doubted very much that God watched over me, the peace of the church, the singing, the gentleness of the priest and Louise seemed important to feel. I turned to my dad.

"Sure, go, kid. Hi Louise. How's Art?"

"He's good, but he's tired of my cookies so I'll make them for Jake."

Again I was dealing with a new school, but the experience was different. Steamer, alias Franklin Taggart, Jr., lived down the street. My dad paid him to cut our lawn or run errands. Steamer took me under his wing. On the second day my dad gave me his charge card and suggested I go with Steamer to buy some decent clothes because it was obvious his ex-wife no longer had any style and let me dress like a slug.

Armed with a new wardrobe, I made an entry into Washington High School with introductions by Steamer. Don't ever let anyone tell you clothes and who you know don't make a difference. They may not make you a better person, but they make a difference in who you meet, how you meet them and what they think of you. From the first day I was accepted as a new member in a large circle of the popular kids that partied hearty. A few of them only showed up at weekend parties, or special occasions, but there was a group of fifteen kids who hung out almost constantly together. I went with them to school dances, house parties, and their nights at the movies where they yelled to each other and threw popcorn through the darkened theatre over the heads of outnumbered patrons. We went to pizza places, hamburger joints, ice skating rinks, bowling alleys, and game centers, always moving around like a swarm, sure of endless spending money, territory and the right to be loud. We pushed our way in, left trash behind us, and especially on weekends, drank until someone passed out.

There wasn't a need to tiptoe quietly through a dark house when I came home. If it was dark the only voice I heard was Roxanne's coming from the couch where she watched television.

"Who's that?" she'd say.

Calling my name usually gave me a free pass to my bedroom without adult inspection. More often the house would still be lit tnd men dressed for business would be coming and going. Dad's voice would boom above everyone's and Roxanne would be looking as bored as she did while watching the news. It was rare that my dad stopped me.

"Hey, Jake, tell everyone what you did at school."

"What?"

"You know, the group you joined. Wait till you hear." A half dozen pairs of eyes turned to look at me.

"Oh, the school yearbook."

"See? Great drive, that boy. Someday he'll own Rupert Murdock."

Chuckles and few thumbs up excused me. A wave from the hallway was all Dad needed.

The school yearbook was my only thread to meeting a quieter group of kids. I helped plan the page layout and organize the photos, but the kids who had worked on the yearbook for a few years did the fun stuff. That didn't matter to me because the only reason I was there was to have a breather. All I wanted was a little time away. I didn't realize it at the time, but the quieter voices and the studious feeling of accomplishment were what I was after. No one in that room was part of the rowdy group with Steamer, and it was my only attempt to get away from them and save myself from my free fall to a dangerous teenage life.

It was about six months after I'd moved to my dad's that a noise woke me. At first I thought it was a car going by that woke me, but then I heard the thud of something hitting the wall in Dad and Roxanne's room. Dad's voice growled, slurring in words I couldn't make out, but I heard Roxanne's animal cry. There were two more dull thuds and then it went quiet.

No one had stirred when I left for school the next morning and both cars were gone when I came back. It was two days before I saw Roxanne when I came home from school. Her bruised face was looking down in the glass of bourbon. Dad wouldn't return for five days.

I went out to sit by the pool and force my head into a school book, though I couldn't concentrate on it. I was wondering about my dad. Who was he? My mom and her family talked about family stories all of the time, but my dad never said a word. I knew he grew up in Steubenville. I knew his mom had died years ago, and that his dad lived in a nursing home up in Akron. He had never asked me to go with him when he went to visit his dad on the third Saturday every other month.

Years before I had watched my dad finish putting on his tie and shoes while he talked to Mom about where he was going. I asked my dad if I could go with him, but he didn't look at me when he said, "You don't need to see any of that, Jake. None of it." After he left, Mom explained that he was embarrassed his father was in a nursing home, and he was only trying to protect me.

I knew that my dad had brothers and sisters, but I didn't know anything about them. Dad had made the men who took care of his laundromat buildings all over the state his friends and family. But while they were his pretend brothers, they were never my uncles. From my room I could hear them talking business, exchanging receipt forms, and discussing purchase orders and repair bills. If I walked by the living room to the kitchen, their serious voices changed, and they talked about football, baseball, or horse racing, though I was never included.

On a Saturday afternoon Louise was waving me over from her back patio. "Jake! Art's not home tonight. Why don't you come in and have his steak?"

"I couldn't do that, Mrs. Bates."

"Sure you can. It will just go to waste. It's too much for me." On previous nights Art hadn't come home for lasagna or spaghetti. "Besides, I want to hear how your mother is doing. I always liked her."

Roxanne, sipping her often watered-down bourbon, (thanks to me), wouldn't miss me. Louise was probably my best friend then. When I did have dinner with her she would tell me stories of growing up in Italy. At church I enjoyed silently sitting beside her, looking at the stained glass windows and listening to the singsong voice of the Father.

When Dad did return after the five days, things changed. What was blustery and loud about him now became blustery, loud, and mean.

"Don't ever wear the same shirt two days in a row, Jake. Do you hear?" I turned to him, surprised he had noticed. "You're a sloth. Go change." Another day he pointed at my school backpack I'd dropped by the door. "Get that damn thing out of here, school boy."

I was asleep on a Tuesday night when he came into my bedroom.

"Wake up."

I stirred, but didn't get up. He grabbed my arm and yanked me straight up. "I said get up. It's time you earned your keep. Get dressed and come downstairs."

When I got to the living room he handed me a brown grocery sack with the heft of books. "Steamer's outside waiting. Give this to who he says."

Steamer was backing out the driveway before I could close the car door. A block away I asked what was going on.

"I don't know."

"Something is."

"Something is and it's none of our business."

I opened the sack to look in.

"You shouldn't do that."

"Why not?"

"If you're caught it's better not to know."

It was money.

Steamer drove us to the parking lot of a cheap twenty-four hour diner. "Over there, see that guy?" A man with white hair was sitting in the driver's seat, a second man was in the back, and a third man was standing by the passenger side of a Buick.

"Yes."

"Give it to him."

Steamer drove up behind the car, put it in neutral and looked at me. I got out and took the bag to the man with the white hair. He put his hand out and I saw a small drool of saliva as he looked at the bag. I was learning that money did funny things to people. I was taller than him, but his arms could have put me down with one swat. He handed the bag to the man in the backseat. After he had looked inside, he nodded.

"Tell your dad he's good with it," the man next to me said.

When we got home Roxanne didn't stir as she watched Johnny Carson. Dad was sitting next to her on the couch with his forearms on his legs, leaning forward to read papers on the coffee table. "Did that small time councilman get his breakfast?" he asked.

"And he thought it was filet mignon for dinner," said Steamer.

I knew Steamer was a favored "neighbor kid," as Dad called him, but it was that night I realized Dad was turning him into his family and friend. From then on Steamer came to see my dad instead of me, and I realized his friendship had always been because of my dad. I started feeling like Steamer's mascot and the only time I went with him anymore was to pick up pizza or dry cleaning. All Steamer wanted to talk about was how he could follow my dad's footsteps in business. He felt so sure of his future that he didn't go to school very often, and I discovered that without him by my side I was invisible as I walked down the hallway between classes.

On weekends when the big parties were held, Steamer picked me up to go, but he'd often disappear with other kids. Insecure and now faced with the truth of who had made me popular and accepted, I wandered through parties talking to a lot of people. I was friends with very few, and I managed to find drink after drink to ease my pain. Usually someone took pity and drove me home, but occasionally I called and begged Roxanne to come. She seldom said anything to me on the way home, unless it was, "Don't get sick in my car."

Over a year went by like this until one night Roxanne, Dad, and I were eating take-out chicken by the pool on a Sunday afternoon when he told me he wanted me to go with Steamer that night to pick up something. The councilman had a new zoning law that needed paying.

"No."

"You can't say no," his eyes popped out like I'd never seen them and his voice bellowed. I noticed a flicker of the kitchen curtain in Louise's house.

"No."

He reached over and grabbed me by the arm.

"Don't do that outside. Everyone can see you," Roxanne's voice was deadpan.

"There isn't a no to me." He let me go and stared at me. No one said a word until he spoke again. "I promised your mother to let you spend your time at school and not make you work."

I looked at him and stopped chewing on my chicken.

"I can see now you'll never be good for work. School's making you soft."

"Oh, Pete, he's just a boy that's been namby-pambied."

"Shut up, Roxanne. Jacob, you're going back to your mother. I can't have you here defying my orders. I let you have everything and you don't appreciate it."

Few of the kids I'd been spending time with at school called to say goodbye, but I also knew I wouldn't miss them. So, with a growing dependence on the friendship of alcohol, I was on a plane the next week on my way back to Washington.

Chapter 9

"Mary, we need eggs and milk."

ALWIDA ARNOLD

My pages of writing were piling up, and the more I wrote, the more confused I became. Gran had asked me to write for Liz, but I was writing things I never wanted Liz to see. How could I ever explain those years of being a confused, hurt, and angry teenager? All that I had taught her would seem a sham. But how could I not honor the love I have for my mother and grandmother by telling my story of being alone and lost through those years? They brought me through it, and the strength of that needed to be made available to Liz.

My help at home was becoming more important, so when possible, I left work early or went in late so I could help Mom and Gran. Gran's health was ever more frail, and Mom was stretched to the limits of her capabilities. She had to help Gran from the bed to her walker, take her to all the doctor visits, and do all the work at home.

Great Party! was going well, but as weeks wore on I was relying more and more on the skill of my team led by Chef Don and Tim. The event for Cameron Enterprises was inching closer, and it was not a good time to be taking any time away. Don and Tim assured me everything was going on schedule and they could handle it.

I was at the office the second week in April when I got the call.

"Jake come now." Mom's voice was deeper than usual and forceful, "I'm in the ambulance with Gran. She was having a hard time breathing and I called. Meet us at the hospital."

My thinking was fuzzy on the way to St. Mark's Hospital. I noticed the beds of red and white tulips around the hospital parking lot, and out of nowhere I remembered the day I jumped over Gran's blooming red tulips in a long thick row by the back porch. Mom and I had only been there a week when I was out playing and recklessly jumped over them, tearing the blooms off half a dozen.

"Jacob! My tulips!" Gran said.

"Jacob! Mother's tulips!" my mom echoed.

Both women's voices had boomed at me as I landed on the grass from the jump.

"Oh, Jake." Pap's deep measured voice was the one that startled me. I'd never heard a man sound so equally calm and firm. "Your grandmother's flowers will always be off limits."

At the hospital I parked in the first space I saw and ran to the emergency room. After I gave Gran's name, a receptionist pointed down the hall, and I turned to run down. To the side, waiting to see which way I was going before joining me, was Logan. I stopped.

"Logan."

"Mr. Buchanan. Your mom called me."

A flash of another moment came to life. I saw myself at his age, three days before Christmas 1987, sitting alone in the hospital corridor where Pap had been rushed. I was waiting for Gran who had told me to sit, and that she wouldn't be long.

"Come along then," I said. We headed down the hall together.

Gran was already stabilized. When we walked in, her tired eyes saw us through the maze of tubes hanging around her. I couldn't tell if she looked at Logan or me first.

Oh, damn, I thought, Logan really is important to her. One more little stray dog she's helped through her life.

We were told she was spending the night at the hospital because her doctor, Dr. Williams, wanted her there. Mom, Logan, and I, listless with relief, sat in a small waiting room on the other side of the hall from Gran. It was ten minutes before anyone said anything.

"Why aren't you in school, Logan?" I asked. Logan looked at Mom for an answer to my question.

"He was, Jake. I got him on his cell phone."

Another five minutes went by. "I'll drive you back to school, Logan. I'm going back to work. Mom, I'll be back at five, and we'll go home when we're sure Gran's fine." Both of them nodded their heads. I kissed Mom on the cheek, and Logan and I headed out.

"I think it's real nice you kissed your mom, Mr. Buchanan."

"When you grow up you don't feel so self-conscious about that anymore, Logan."

"I used to kiss my mom, but it's been a long time."

"What do you and Gran talk about?"

"Mostly her husband. She still misses him a lot, doesn't she?"

"Yes. She does."

"She tells me about the kitchen cupboards he built, and how he made her move to a dump with a raccoon living in the fireplace."

"They lived in a twenty-four foot motor home at the time, not in a dump. Besides, the dump was later turned into a beautiful house. And you've heard that story before."

"Yes."

"What else do you talk about?"

"What a cute boy you were. How you loved her lobster casserole on Saturday nights and the pizza that Matt hated."

"Why does all that interest you, Logan?" I asked. We were now pulled over to the curb by his school.

He looked away from me. His thin shoulders didn't look like they got much more food than the extra sandwiches he might eat at work. "I don't know, Mr. Buchanan."

"Yes, you do. Why?"

"I think because, well, because I've never heard stories like that. My grandma never told me stories about when I was little."

I remembered that his had died, and I felt guilty for making him remember. "Anything else?"

"They make me feel good. I would have liked to be you. With a mom and grandparents."

That was too much to hear from an employee. "Alright, Logan. You better get back to class."

From that day on it felt like a shadow followed me as I watched Gran's health decline. Gran's rush to the hospital coupled with dealing with a confused, unhappy teenage boy made past events rush back to me in a slap of emotion that followed me through the days and often showed up in alternately uneasy and comforting dreams.

Gran ended up having to stay three nights in the hospital to monitor her erratic heartbeat and blood pressure. On the third night, Mom and I were having a late supper of Chinese food I'd picked up on the way home. I was spending my days at work with an early and late stop at the hospital, and Mom was spending all day at the hospital. The ham fried rice and whatever else I got with it weren't good, but we sat there eating anyway.

"Jake, Dr. Williams came to the waiting room to talk to me after he'd seen Mother. He didn't flinch, he looked me in the eye and said, 'Your mother's heart problems are catching up with her, and the leukemia is soon going to keep her in bed.' He said we needed to think about hospice."

"Do you remember when Pap died, Mom?"

"I've been thinking about that a lot these past few days."

"When he collapsed for the last time you tried to resuscitate him."

"Yes, Gran ran to the phone to call 911 while I worked on him. I remember. I can still remember the smell of beef ribs and potatoes in the oven that night."

"You kept him alive."

"I tried. But it wasn't enough."

"It was enough until the paramedics came. His last heart attack. Poor Pap. Between the diabetes and his heart, we didn't know which one would take him."

"Gran never recovered. You may not remember, but she's never been quite the same, quite as happy. You know what she told me last week?"

"What?"

"She wondered if Matt had forgotten about her: if he was in heaven and so busy that he's just forgotten about her."

"I don't think that would happen."

"Neither do I and I told her so."

These talks with Mom were the little comfort I had during that time because the writing I was making myself do and the dreams I didn't want would sometimes be confused in my thinking. Logan weaved in and out of my dreams, and sometimes he seemed to stand outside of my thoughts while I wrote late in the night.

The next day Mom drove Gran home, and Gran was on the phone when I came home two hours later. Shadow was wagging his tail at her feet. When she hung up she was beaming. "Guess who that was?"

"I couldn't guess."

"Good Time Klair. I haven't talked to her since last summer."

"How is she?"

"Still selling real estate. It's a miracle she's still around. She started talking about the great Christmases we used to have. Do you remember, Jake?"

"Yes."

"She reminded me of the Christmas you came back after you were at your dad's, that old coot."

"Oh."

"You looked half revved and ready to fight hell for entry."

"Not an easy time being a teenager."

"I remember we were all so worried about you when you got home looking angry and hurt at the same time."

"Okay, enough of me."

"No. Never too much of you. On the way home after we picked you up from the airport I started complaining to Matt. 'What are we going to do? He's all screwed up, again.' And Matt said, 'Love him like we did last time. He'll come around.'"

"He wasn't so bad, Mom. He was just a teenager," my mom said.

"For a few moments a near worthless one."

"Thanks, Gran," I said.

"Don't want you too full of yourself. You with your own company and all. Look at you now," she sighed. "I've got to go to bed. I'm exhausted."

Mom and I helped her to her room, then I left Mom and Shadow to help her get ready for bed. Mom has put every one of us to bed. Gran, Pap, Dad, Liz, me, and even Shadow when he was a puppy.

When I went back to the kitchen I saw the note Gran had written with Klair's phone number. I took my phone out of my pocket and called. "Hi, Klair, another voice from the past here."

We talked about nothing for a few minutes, and she lamented the loss of another Christmas tree farm in the area to a developer even though it would be positive for the real estate market.

"Klair, I've got something to ask you," I said.

"Really?"

"Yes, I want you to keep your eye open. Tell me if it looks like Gran's old place comes up for sale. I might be interested."

"Well, lordy be. I'll do some prying, but I know you wouldn't find it in the fine shape Alwida and Matt left it. The current owners aren't near so neat."

The next day was Saturday, but I went in to make sure that plans for the night's Great Party! event were running smoothly as we prepared to feed a hundred at a local wedding reception center. I helped for an hour, expending nervous energy and assuring myself that the client would be well served.

"You know that Logan?" Tim was talking as he rearranged the food shelf and took inventory.

"Yes."

"I overheard the kids talking. He's spending his nights at the homeless shelter on Second South. Poor kid. I don't know his story, but that's no place for a teenager. No wonder he's the first in line to eat leftover food around here."

Dean Martin was crooning from a stereo when I walked in the back door at home an hour later. As soon as Gran saw me, she turned from the crossword puzzle she was working on and called to Mom. "Mary, come here."

"Yes?"

"Mary, we need eggs and milk."

"We have eggs and milk, Mother."

"Mary, we need eggs and milk and take your time looking around the grocery store." Gran's eyes were fixed on me looking for agreement to the conspiracy, and Mom gave a daughter's shrug of resignation and went for her purse.

I got up to start water for tea while we waited for Mom to leave. The sound of her car had faded down the block when Gran spoke. "I need a seven letter word for a thorough search among confusing objects."

"What did you want to talk about, Gran?"

"Let's not rush into it too quickly. Mary will be a while."

"Okay. Darjeeling tea or some kind of herbal?"

"Give me the real stuff."

"I need your help with something, too," I said. "I talked with Liz yesterday, and Ann got on the phone and asked me, if you can believe it, to get your help in finding her non-existent box."

"Why me?"

"She said you'd remember since you seem to remember everything else."

"I remember she could have been a better mother and changed Liz's diapers more often. Do you remember that rash Liz got?"

"Yes, but that was a long time ago and she got it cleared up."

"Still." She wrote something on the crossword puzzle, and then looked at me, now sitting across from her with the steaming teacups between us. "You're going to have a harder time being a father, a good father, with all this distance between the two of you."

"Yes, I know."

"I'm having a harder time being a grandmother and I haven't much time left to be one."

"Oh, Gran, you could well see Liz married."

"No, I won't, Jacob, and we both know that. You heard the doctor. Face the facts. That's why I wanted to talk to you." She looked down and took her tea bag out, squeezed hot dark tea out of it and put it to the side of the cup. "We all have a time in life when we have to face the facts. You can't run forever."

"No, you can't." My mind flashed back to the day Ann walked out of our marriage.

"You've had a couple of bad times and so have I. Now is one of those times. I have to decide what is truly important to leave in life. When Clive Stewart left Mary and me to go to California when she was only ten weeks old, that was the hardest. Those days we were alone in that godforsaken apartment out in the middle of nowhere were the hardest days of my life. There was only a baby I didn't know, or know how to take care of, the radio, and every day less and less food."

She stopped to drink her tea and I didn't say anything. "But Jake, it gave me time to face the facts, and when I did that, I knew what I needed to do."

"Yes."

"That man left me with nothing. Left his own baby with nothing. But I would never let that happen again and I knew it was up to me to always, *always* be strong."

"You are strong, Gran."

"I made myself strong. Strong enough to go to school in New York alone. I learned to face those numbers on ledgers and find every nickel, every penny, so I would always have a way to make a living without anyone else."

"And you did."

"I did. For years, I did. Years before all that women's lib stuff."

I smiled remembering Gran's remarks when she would watch television during the movement's bra burning days. "Look at those spoiled white women who need approval from the very people they say they want to be free of. They should just go out and do it! No one's going to help you do what you have to do yourself."

"But, Jake, here's what I want to tell you," I looked at her. "First, there's a story about my mother, Pauline. By the time I knew her father, my grandfather, he was a slow moving, clumsy, old man, but when he was younger he was a raging alcoholic who squandered an inheritance from Belgium and beat his wife. See that? Too much beating of women in this family. He came home drunk and hit grandma, but what he didn't see coming was his nine-year old daughter, Pauline, behind him who grabbed a hot skillet with a tea towel, climbed up on a chair and hit him on the back of the skull. It left a burn mark with no hair for the rest of his life."

"No, I haven't heard that story."

"Except for the ungrateful Annieconda, and she isn't our blood, every woman down the line has been beat or left by men."

"Not a good legacy. And you were beaten, too."

"Exactly the point. That's what you have to pass on to Liz. Don't let her continue this cycle. You broke it and she needs to know that and know she can't ever be hit. She can't ever allow that."

"Gran, I've been doing something you told me to do."

"You should be doing a lot of things I told you to do."

"Gran," I paused, hoping I could say this right, "I've

been working to write up your story like you've told me to. I've been telling mine, too, and it hasn't been easy."

"Is that what you've been doing on the computer at night?"

"Yes."

She smiled and turned to the crossword puzzle. "Look at this word, Jake, what could it be? Seven letters that mean a thorough searching among confusing objects."

I thought the talk session was over, so I started gathering the teacups when she grabbed my hands and held them closed between us.

"But there's something else, too, Jake."

I watched her.

"Something else just as important. Knowing when to love."

I knew who she meant. Anyone who knew her would. "Gran, why did you love Pap so much?"

"He was a good, *good* man." Her voice ached with longing.

Later that evening as I watched television my mind wandered to the puzzle Gran was leaving me. How do I tell Liz, teach Liz, how to choose wisely? How can anyone know who will hit and who will love? Rummage. That was the word we never thought of on the crossword puzzle. To look through confusing objects is to rummage through them, whether it is a messy kitchen drawer or your own life.

Chapter 10

"Please, God, don't take him. He's my life."
ALWIDA ARNOLD

Earth was continuing to spring to life outside with hyacinths, daffodils, and tulips replacing the forsythia's now dropped, faded, yellow petals. That's the bare skinny-branched shrub I was staring out the window at when the idea came to me.

"Mom, what do you think?" I whispered the idea to her before Gran came out of her room in the morning.

"I think it's a great idea. I'll get the decorations out this afternoon."

The morning was spent bent over bids which were becoming so numerous I decided it was time to finally hire an assistant. When I brought it up to Chef Don and Tim during a noon-time scheduling session they both jumped on it like I should have decided on it months ago.

I wanted to leave by four o'clock, so I buckled down to finish the bids and make phone calls right after lunch. At 4:15, I decided to put it all away whether it was finished or not. There would be a tomorrow for all the papers on my desk; what I didn't know was if Gran had a tomorrow.

I walked to the back where everyone was bustling like they should be and went over to Tim. "I'm taking Logan with me to run errands and then taking him home. Mark him on duty until five."

"Done. If you're around any paper towels pick up a few rolls. My shipment's not coming in for two days."

I motioned Logan over to me and told him I wanted him to help with an errand and I'd take him home after. He turned faster than a jackrabbit to get his backpack and waved goodbye to Melissa who was watching.

Once inside the car and on our way, I told him we were on our way to a garden nursery. He didn't ask any questions, just stared ahead. I waited for a song to end on the radio.

"Aren't you curious why, Logan?"

"Not really. Maybe it's centerpieces."

"You should be curious. Always be curious about your own life, Logan, and what you're doing."

He turned to look at me.

"Learn to think about your life. It'll help you in the long run to see what's really going on."

He still hadn't asked anything when we were inside the nursery filled with blooming bulb plants and flats of summer flowers that wouldn't be sold for another month. "We're going to the back to look at potted trees," I said.

Once in front of the trees it was time to explain.

"We're picking out a Christmas tree. This weekend is going to be Christmas for Gran and we want the most beautiful tree here."

His eyes grew, then slowly narrowed as he began studying the trees. He looked at them with eyes I hadn't seen before. There was a thread of life making its way out. Logan walked around all the trees and studied several from different angles. I made my own way through them while keeping an eye on him. I may never have a son, I thought.

"Can I help you with a tree?" a female voice came from behind.

"If you could get a cart for us to put a tree on that would be helpful."

As she walked away I turned to Logan, "See one you like?"

"This one, Mr. Buchanan. I think this one."

It was a seven foot balsam fir, thick, glossy, and a perfect cone. "That's one I noticed, too. We'll take it. Here, help me put it on the dolly."

The kid that drove with me in the car from Great Party! to the nursery was not the same kid who was in the car with me to the house. He smiled, there was a blush on his face, a corny gleam in his eye and he twitched a little dance of happiness in his seat.

"Really, Mr. Buchanan, you're going to have Christmas for Ms. Alwida?" He was moving his hands so much that I noticed them. They were raw, chaffed.

"Yes, I thought the house needed a little happiness, or what it could get, anyway."

"Wow. I've never heard of doing that."

"Christmas was always really important to Gran."

"Cool," he leaned back and seemed to be sorting memories of what Gran had told him. He sat up and said, "Have you got a bottle of White Shoulders?"

"Well, no, I haven't, but I know where we can get one." We stopped at Rite-Aid before going home.

As I turned onto the street outside the store, I asked, "What happened to your hands, Logan?"

"Oh, nothing. They get cold, you know. You can let me out here unless there's something else you want me to do." We were at a strip mall I knew was several miles from his home.

"Listen, Logan, you've been a good friend for Gran. Unless you have somewhere else you need to be, why don't you come home with me now and help us trim the tree."

His grin was my answer, but all that crossed my mind was wondering what in the world I was doing bringing an underage employee home with me to decorate a Christmas tree in April. Mom had cleared the space out in the living room and had a dozen boxes of ornaments lined up against the wall. Gran was on the couch looking wan and pale with pillows propping her up and a blanket pulled to her chin. She smiled when I walked in, but she lit up when she saw Logan trailing behind me.

Mom had the Christmas music ready to start with our traditional favorites of Frank Sinatra, Dean Martin, Bing Crosby, Rosemary Clooney, Ella Fitzgerald, and a little Bobby Darin thrown in.

"This music is going to blow your mind, boy, so buckle up and enjoy," Gran told Logan.

When I stopped drinking it was a long time before I realized normal people could get a feeling of near intoxicating pleasure without drinking at all. This evening in April of 2010 was one of those moments. As I stood on the step stool holding strings of light and taking direction from Mom on how to cascade them around, my mind began to walk quietly through memories of all the years we had put together beautiful trees. Mom closed the drapes and we turned on lamps so Gran could inspect our work before the bows and ornaments were placed. She directed Logan and me to adjust first here and then there, and admonished us to make sure the quality was as good on the side she couldn't see. "I know the standards of both of you leave a bit to be desired, so check carefully."

Shadow, who was curled by Gran's feet, lifted his head and gave a long sound of support to her accusation before putting down his head again to watch our clumsy moves.

Mom went to the kitchen to make dinner, leaving Logan and me to be directed by Gran in placement of bows and then ornaments. I felt suspended in time, enjoying every moment as Logan and I traded off. He wasn't, and never would be Liz, but he was young, and I could see for this moment in time he was important to this family. His eyes darted from one to the other of us for direction, his movements were quick and seemed to anticipate what would be asked of him next, like where to put the next clear glass ornament from the 1950's that had been so gently tucked away only three months earlier. He had not made a phone call to report to anyone where he was. No one was waiting for him.

We took a break for dinner before Gran's final inspection. I helped Gran to the table, Logan held her chair, and we both scooted her in. Before he sat down, Logan slipped into the living room and put the *White Shoulders* deep in the tree branches. Mom had created the season with traditional roast ham and potatoes, cranberries, green beans with almonds, and an orange, avocado and romaine salad.

"This is beautiful," Logan whispered to no one.

After everyone was served, conversation casually resumed and then turned to what was going on at Great Party! Both Logan and I gave a re-creation of how all of the equipment that was needed for an event was packed away in the minivan in a certain order that Chef Don unfailingly closely directed.

Dean Martin was crooning in the background as I continued, "He's going to be gone tomorrow, he's taking his daughter's class on a field trip to Timpanagos Cave."

"He's a good dad. I've seen pictures of his kids and wife," said Logan.

"They didn't have all these field trips when Jake was in school or Matt would have taken him," Gran said.

"Yes, Matt was a good dad, too," said Mom. "He was a good dad to me and we didn't have field trips either, though I was in junior high when he came along."

"Logan, tell Jake about your dad." Gran's voice was a directive.

He looked down and for the first time held his fork still. The chafe on his knuckle looked like it was ready to split the dry skin. "He died two years ago. He was a good dad, too."

"Logan's dad died three days after a car accident."

"My mom and I miss him a lot. She's got somebody else now, but it's not the same."

Mom swerved the conversation, "Jake, now it's your turn. Tell Logan about your first Christmas back from Ohio when you were seventeen."

"Yes, I want to hear you talk about my Matthew," Gran added.

My first Christmas back from Ohio was the story that had been returning to me while decorating the tree. Moments had flashed a dozen times about that Christmas of 1987. But now that I was asked to retell it, how much could I? How much could I say to this boy sitting beside me who was suffering much the same as I had that year? I decided to start with the honesty of what I was like as a teenager.

"I had come back from my father's house in Ohio in April that year. My dad beat my mom, that's why we left. He beat this second wife, too. Even so, it hurt to leave my dad, but I didn't mind leaving the school there, not at all, though the new school in Washington wasn't any better. I was a lost kid."

Logan looked up at me a bit surprised, but I decided to give him the full story. "I was seventeen when I left my dad's house the second time. It was an ugly situation and he wanted me gone. I was in with a rough crowd and drinking heavily. Back in Washington, Mom and her second husband Ron had split up. I don't know what happened in that split up, but I know she never went by his name again. She settled on Buchanan so we would have the same last name. She was now living about ten miles from Gran and Pap, and still working two jobs, so I was left to make my own way.

"I knew I wouldn't like the new school any better than I had the last few and I didn't try to like it. I wore my hair long like you, Logan, and made myself feel cool in my leather jacket and acid washed jeans. I didn't have any belief in myself and I didn't think I had anyone who really cared. Mom did, but I ignored her, and fought with her whenever she tried to say anything, and I thought I'd outgrown my grandparents. I thought grandparents were for little boys, and I wasn't one anymore. I hadn't seen them in months though we only lived the ten miles apart. What friends I had were as mixed up as me, but we all knew how to find booze and drink and party and try to forget. I didn't like where I was, but I didn't know what to do. I felt like a fake, a poser trying to look normal, damaged goods not worth loving.

"It all began the morning of December 21st. School was out for Christmas, and I'd been out the night before and came home drunk. I was sleeping it off when Mom came in to wake me up. She moved my shoulders and ran her fingers through my hair. 'Jacob, get up. You need to get dressed and go help Gran get ready for Christmas.'

"I tried to push her away, but it didn't work. 'Matt's in the hospital. He had another heart attack and he's still got pneumonia. She had to call an ambulance last night. You need to go spend the day with her and help.' I didn't want to go, but I wasn't being given a choice, so I got up and Mom got me over there about an hour later, and dropped me off without any means of escape.

"Gran was a darting, nervous queen bee when I arrived. She was fluttering around and moving so much to keep busy, she started to make me dizzy. She'd been so upset that she'd forgotten to fix Grandma Pauline's tea. That was my first job: to make tea and toast for Grandma Pauline and take it her bed. Then she had a million things for me to do, didn't you, Gran?"

"And you weren't doing them fast enough. Matt had been recovering from pneumonia for weeks, so I'd spent my time running back and forth to work and taking Matt to doctor appointments and making him comfortable.

That pneumonia on top of his diabetes and heart problems wasn't making him any better and the doctors weren't helping at all. The night before, he woke in the night wheezing and grabbing his chest, so I called an ambulance. Christmas had been put aside and this was my last chance to get the house right so when he came home it would be ready for him."

I picked up when she stopped talking. "She was throwing out the orders of what I needed to do. Move the furniture to make room for a tree, clean the floor, bring in the boxes of ornaments from where she'd left them in the barn after taking them out of the storage space. I strung lights out on the front porch, put doodads on the coffee table, and finally got a sandwich as payment."

"There wasn't time for anything else, Jake. We had to go get a tree. I didn't have the tree up yet! That's the latest I'd ever waited."

Mom got up from the table and began cutting blueberry pie and topping it with ice cream. Logan was listening so intently she needed to tap him on the shoulder to get his attention to pass it around. "Then what happened, Mr. Buchanan?"

"Gran told me to get in the truck and we headed to the K-Mart to buy a tree. There wasn't much of a selection three days before Christmas. We ended up with a straggly Charlie Brown that neither of us liked, but it was the best they had. I strapped it in the truck bed while Gran ran in the store to buy a few items. When she came back we headed home to decorate.

"All day I'd followed directions from Gran to pull out ornaments from the storage space in the barn attic, wipe them off, clear away furniture and follow her around at the K-Mart ugly Christmas tree lot. Gran tried to talk to me while we decorated the tree with the ornaments I'd bothered to bring in the house because they were the first ones I found, but I didn't respond much. I was too busy paying attention to myself. When Gran stopped decorating so we could get to the hospital, Grandma Pauline laughed at the tree saying, 'Alwida, that's the saddest damn thing I've ever seen.' She just glared at her mother as daughters so often do.

"It was late afternoon before we went to see Matt at Harbor View Hospital. I can still remember walking down that hospital hall. My boots had that dull, thick sound on the old linoleum and I told myself I was the only cool looking person in a ten mile radius. The bleach and disinfectant smell of that old place still comes back to me when I walk through a hospital.

"Gran's step was setting the pace, and I was irritated with her for dragging me around for what felt like hours, making me work, and not letting me go home. I thought I'd done enough grandson duty for the day and I didn't want to be in that stinky place that smelled like old people and sickness. When she asked if I wanted see Pap, I said no. She looked angry, but she also didn't want to waste time talking about it.

"'You wait here, Jake,' she said to me, pointing at a bench at the end of a hall. She went off on her own, and I sat down, pissed at being there and relieved I didn't have to go with her."

"My Matthew looked so frail" Gran said and continued, "When I walked in his room I wanted to wail. Wail like those old women you see on television crying over the dead in the Middle East. He had tubes coming out all over and his hair, thick and short as his hair was, poked out in ways I'd never seen. I was sure they'd hurt him and I was angry at everyone. But the second I sat down next to him and he opened his eyes and saw me, saw me like the first time he ever looked at me with those deep brown sugar eyes, I only wanted to beg God to let him rest and sleep well and return to me." Gran's chest rose and fell like she was reliving the moment one more time. "His eyes smiled love at me, then closed again in sleep."

Logan hadn't touched his pie. I needed to finish the story; it was getting late. "Meanwhile, I was back on the bench. It was a hard one, too, and there wasn't a television nearby, and no one sat beside me to talk to, so my mind began to drift. It wasn't often I let myself think about life in those years. Flashes of scenes went in and out of my mind. No words to them, just short scenes. I remembered Pap showing me how to hold the new red chain saw he bought me. I remembered the bumpy truck rides on Saturday morning to the Kingston Ferry Docks to buy crab and then for several seconds I saw Gran and

Pap dancing in the kitchen after dinner to Rosemary Clooney music, and I could see their arms around each other and hear the song. Those were happy moments.

"There I was, that surly kid who didn't want to be there, and out of nowhere I felt a slight turn in my mood to a softness I didn't recognize. It startled me so much I sat up and shook myself out of the feelings. I wondered why Gran was taking so long, and again I became irritated that I was there at all. You know why I finally got up from that hard bench to walk down the hall? I was wondering what could possibly be taking so long. I wanted to get out of there and away from the hospital. I didn't want my heart to soften. I walked down the hallway to the room on the right where Gran had disappeared, but I stopped short at the doorway. The only light in the room was a lamp on a bedside table. The soft light circled Pap's gaunt face and haloed the back of Gran's head. He was sleeping and she sat holding and kissing his hand. Then she whispered, 'Please God, don't take him, he's my life. Please God, don't let him die.'"

"He was my life, Logan, he still is. I miss him."

"Seeing Gran pray, the anger I had felt walking toward that room evaporated as though it never existed. I was humbled like I had never, ever felt. Then I did something I hadn't done since I was nine and Mom and I left Dad. I returned to the bench, sat down, put my forearms on my legs, closed my hands together, bent my head, and whispered, 'Please, God, don't let him die.'"

Chapter 11

*"That's the past, and there's no going back.
There's only forward."*

Alwida Arnold

I know it's not smart for an employer to bring home an underage employee, but that night, after a pretend Christmas, I also knew I couldn't let a seventeen-year-old boy out into the streets with no place to go. I asked him where he wanted me to take him, but when he hesitated, Gran announced, "He can stay here. I'm inviting him. Mary, we have extra blankets for the couch, don't we?"

Reluctantly, I left the two women to fuss while I went to my area of the house. Between the two of them, I'd been saved years ago. Maybe one night could help Logan face his challenges.

The next morning I left for the office while it was still dark. I didn't look toward the living room when I left, but Mom called at seven and said Logan had neatly folded his sheet and blankets and left without a word before she was up. At ten Ann called.

"Have you found the box? And where is your support payment? I haven't received it yet."

"Well, good morning to you, too, Ms. Annieconda," I wanted to add, but didn't.

"Look, I'm strapped for money here. We live in a two income world and your daughter and I are living on one."

"Is that all you want, Ann?"

"No. Well, yes, but we'll get through this small talk. Have you found the box?"

"Why in hells bells do you want that box, and why should I look for it again?"

She sighed and her voice went into a lower, softer gear, surprising me. "All right. I'll tell you. I want that box because it has a few things in it that are important to me."

"What?"

"It's really none of your business, but just for the hell-a-vit, I'll tell you. It has two mementos that mean a lot to me, and I want to pass them on to Liz."

"That's all you're going to say?"

"That's all you need to know."

"I haven't got time to look. Gran's losing strength, and she and Mom are my first priority."

The conversation continued to the bitter end. I had forgotten to pay, or rather the cash flow had been tight and I'd made my choice to make payroll rather than send Ann money, but I had gotten a good size check two days earlier, so I told her it would be out that day.

I didn't want Liz to be without, but juggling today's business finances well would also make a difference for her in the long run.

Logan reported for his shift that day, but when we passed going opposite directions we didn't even glance at each other. It was around five when there was a gentle knock on my office door.

"Come in."

"Hi Mr. Buchanan, Tim said to bring this in to you." Todd, Logan's friend, set down a standard size box emblazoned with, "Stay out! This means you. Annie's box!"

"Where was that?"

"In the back corner of the storage room. We were getting so low on paper towels that it just showed up." He turned to go.

"Todd, just a minute."

He turned and waited.

"Todd, where's Logan staying now?"

"He stays at my house on weekends, but my Mom thinks he's home during the week. My dad's out of work so I know they're having trouble with money. I give most my check to them."

"Where is he during the week?"

"Sometimes he does go home. His mom wants him there. He doesn't have a cell phone anymore, so she calls me about him."

"Oh."

"His Mom's got to leave that man. He's bad. A few times Logan's crawled in my bedroom window and slept on the floor without my parents knowing. Or he goes to the shelter. Once I stayed in the bathroom with him so my parents would think it was me taking a shower. Then I had to sneak him out."

I nodded, excusing him, and then stared at the closed door. I hated hearing about the lives of my youngest employees. Don and Tim were family men. The college students were working for a future. But the teens were working to survive. And sometimes it felt like they all looked to me as some kind of father and I'm not their father. I'm not.

As I drove home that night I purposely noticed that spring was renewing the earth with green grass, budding trees, and bright, blooming bulb flowers. For a moment it made me forget about the heavy feeling of impending death at home. It was comforting to notice the lengthening, brighter days. As I pulled into the driveway, the twinkling lights of a Christmas tree brought me back to the deepness and mystery of winter, God, and the scale of human life.

Gran was weakening with each day. The returned leukemia sapped her strength, her heart continued to struggle, and her crumbling spine made her a frail, delicate snowflake. Each day she was heavier for my tired mother to lift and move about for her basic needs. Shadow was also aware of the short time Gran would be with us. He parked himself by her and seldom left. He didn't even greet me at the door unless it was late at night when Gran was deeply asleep.

On a Tuesday I got home as the sun was setting. When I walked in the door I smelled the delicious scent of roast duck and rose Louise. The china was arranged on the tablecloth and new candlesticks waited to be lit. Ella Fitzgerald was singing and happy voices were talking in the living room.

"What's going on here?" I asked. Mom, Gran, and Logan turned to look at me.

"Jake! At last you're here. We've been waiting," said Mom.

"For what?"

"The tree undressing ceremony, and then Gran says she has an announcement."

"Ms. Alwida asked me to come over and help, Mr. Buchanan," Logan walked to the empty ornament boxes lined up against the far wall to start helping now that I was here.

I walked to the tree and peered deeply into the middle of it. "Before we do that, we need to do one more thing. Gran, you need to come over here and look for something."

"Oh, yes!" Logan's eyes were as bright with the remembered surprise as Gran's.

After Logan and I helped Gran over in the walker she leaned slightly from side to side while she looked through the branches. "I see something. I see it."

I nodded to Logan and he reached in and pulled out the box.

"Ah, White Shoulders. Oh, Jake, you remembered even in April." Her eyes filled and a tear slowly slipped down her cheek.

Later we were finishing a dessert of cheesecake when Mom asked, "What's the announcement, Mom? We've eaten dinner and you haven't said a thing."

Regally, Gran lifted her shoulders and looked into the eyes of each of us. "Shadow and I have decided it's time for hospice."

For some silly reason we all looked at Shadow who was sitting by Gran for an explanation. He lifted his head and wagged his tail.

"Hospice? You want to go there?" Mom asked.

"Yes, dear, I do. I most definitely do. It is my decision, after all." Mom and I began talking in confused sentences while Logan listened. Though she didn't say it directly, I think it was because she could see how tired, worn, and frail my mother, her only child, was becoming because of the need to care for her.

There was a deepening realization of Gran's situation when Mom and I began looking for a hospice. We settled on Forest Grove Home, about five miles from home. We took her in on a Saturday afternoon. Efficient, cheery, and kind people welcomed her to the last home she would have. Sadie Morgan, a red-haired and round woman in her late forties, introduced herself as Gran's head nurse who would be watching her closely. She took over the wheelchair, leaving Mom and me to trail behind. Sadie knew that Gran had lived in Washington and said that she hoped they would have time to talk about what a beautiful state it is. "Yes," said Gran, "we'll spend at least one afternoon talking about fresh crab that no native Utahn knows a twit about."

Once Gran was settled in bed Sadie disappeared to other duties, and Mom went to sign papers and go over medications. I sat by Gran with my chest throbbing with the pain of leaving her here. She took my hand, "It's okay, dear, don't be sad."

"Gran, I've talked to Klair a couple of times since she called you. She's doing some covert inquiries to see if I could buy your old house in Bothell."

She rubbed my hand, "Oh, honey, that's sweet. But, dear Jake, don't do it. Don't buy it. That's the past and there's no going back. There's only forward. That's why I chose to come here."

"But, Gran . . ."

"No, dear, only forward. I learned that when Clive Stewart left your mother and me. That's what kept me alive and you need to hear this and release yourself to always go forward. It was going forward that gave me Matt."

I looked down at the floor, unsure of what to say. She still held my hand, but she slowly took it away. "I have to go forward."

"Pap will be waiting for you, Gran."

"Do you think so, Jake? Really?"

"Yes."

"It's been so long since I've seen him. Maybe he's forgotten me."

"No, Gran, he couldn't do that. I know he couldn't."

Mom walked into the room. "Mom, is there anything I can go to the store to get you? Something you need?"

"No, dear, just sit with me here a little while longer."

Chapter 12

*"Mary's learned to be strong,
and her soul strength is in her gentle heart."*
ALWIDA ARNOLD

The house was emptier with Gran at hospice. Mom and I knew it would be though we said little about it.

"I do miss seeing Logan from time to time. He doesn't come to see me," Mom said. We were having breakfast on the first Saturday in May.

"Well, he shouldn't. In the end, he's an employee."

"And a human being."

"Yes, but fraternizing is a dangerous thing."

"Jake, he needs help. He's a boy. I wish I could have him stay here for a year."

"Oh, Mom. He's got his own family."

"Don't forget how the time you spent with your grandparents changed you when our life was so confusing and difficult. Jake, kindnesses need to continue. A couple of times when I've gone to sit with Mom he's been there, so I know how much they mean to each other."

I was powerless to end the visits, and I didn't really want to, so I stopped asking about them.

Mom decided to visit a friend and catch up on a few errands that afternoon since I was going to spend most of it sitting with Gran. When I got there she was dressed and waiting.

"It's about time you came to visit."

"I didn't know I had an appointed time."

"You do. My chosen time. Bring the car around, Jeeves, because we're going to O. C. Tanner."

"What?"

"You heard me." It was a surprise to see her looking so perky and ready to shop, plus the most expensive jewelry store in Salt Lake was an extravagance. On our way I learned she had several missions to accomplish with this spree.

"You're strong, Jake."

"What?"

"I said you're strong. You always have been. Not everyone in this family has been."

"You are."

"Yes, I am and so are you. My mother wasn't. She suffered from too many weaknesses of spirit. And men who leave their women and babies, well, they are the very weakest."

"And Mom?"

"Mary's learned to be strong, and her soul strength is in her gentle heart. Jake, promise me something."

"What?"

"You must always take care of your mother. Don't ever leave her behind. She needs you."

Traffic was light enough that I could glance for a long second at Gran, "I promise."

"Good. Now that that's settled, let's shop!"

We were browsing along the dinner rings display when I finally thought to ask what she was looking to buy.

"Something for your mother."

"Oh."

"Mother's Day is coming up, and I don't have anything yet. This is the last Mother's Day I will be able to give my baby a present." Slowly, deliberately, and with great pleasure Gran savored trying ring after ring on her old, skinny fingers. For over an hour she enjoyed admiring diamonds, rubies, topaz, emeralds and a dozen other gems. The softness of her eyes told me she was remembering how Pap would surprise her with rings for Christmas and her birthday. "They would look much better on my daughter's hand, but she's not near as good at picking them out as I am," she told the salesman.

Finally she settled on an amethyst and diamond ring that was secured in a blue velvet box and wrapped in heavy coated white paper with gold grosgrain ribbon. "There! Mission accomplished. Thanks for paying for a Mother's Day present from me."

"You're welcome."

"Don't forget to buy one from you."

"Okay, I won't."

"One more thing." Apparently not all missions had been accomplished in the jewelry store. "Jake, I want you to be kind to Logan. I know he is an employee. You've told me a hundred times, but more important than that, he's a young man who needs help like you did, and I want you to watch out for him."

"Between you and Mom it looks like I don't have a choice."

"Good."

Mother's Day was the next weekend and we brought Gran home for a barbecue. The first thing she did after settling herself on a lounge chair with the sun on her face, was give the small wrapped box to Mom.

"Oh, Mom, it's beautiful," Mom nearly squealed. "But it's too expensive."

"Yes, and that's why Jake paid for it. But it's from me, not him at all."

"Thank you, Mom."

My gift to Mom from the designer department in Nordstrom was already hanging in the closet. The personal shopper at the store made it the easiest shopping for a woman I'd ever done.

The second thing Gran did was ask where Logan was. Mom answered, "As we were about to walk out the door to pick you up he called and said he wouldn't be over for the barbecue because he was spending the day with his mother."

"I'm going to miss the boy," said Gran.

I didn't say anything, but I was surprised to discover I felt that way, too. He wasn't a bad person to have around if I couldn't have Liz. Still, Gran, Mom and I have a long history of the three of us eating meals together, and we had a good time that afternoon. A few of Gran's old friends dropped by, and she received a call from Klair and Margie who had worked at Padgett's Pharmacy, and surprisingly from Lawrence who still owned the Christmas Tree Farm in Carnation, Washington.

"Lots of old voices," she said.

"Old voices who still remember and love you."

"It's time to go, Jake, I need to get back to bed." Her wording was so startling that I wondered at first if she meant to Washington to visit friends, but I quickly knew she meant she wanted to get back to her bed at Forest Grove. "Sadie will be angry with me if I'm too tired to tell her stories tomorrow."

Mom looked in my eyes, and I knew we were both slipping into a *deja vu* shadow world of when Matt was so very ill that he, too, spent most of his time in bed. In the end, he had a last heart attack and lost consciousness minutes before dinner was to be served. On a Tuesday evening, Gran was about to serve and Mom was helping him to the table when he fell from her hold, landing heavily on the floor. She frantically began CPR while Gran dialed 911. The next day the doctor told Gran that only the machines were keeping breath moving through him. She spent the night with him, and at 5:30 a.m.

she, *not* a doctor or nurse, disconnected the machine as Washington law required.

That evening, with Gran well tucked into her bed at Forest Grove, Mom reading in her room, and Shadow at my feet, I sat at the computer. For a few minutes I attempted to do some catch up work for the office, but I could not think about it. My mind would not focus on crunching numbers, preparing bids, and suggesting party ideas. Even the looming Cameron Enterprises event felt inconsequential at the moment. I opened the file where I had been writing Gran's story. Still, all I did was stare at the blinking cursor.

"Before I write this part of the story, I need to tell it. I need to share it with someone I know who needs it. Someone who is ready to understand it," I said aloud. I wondered when I would see Logan again.

The next days continued with a quality of the dark hours of night when everything is still, but for some reason you wake and the only thing you hear is your own heartbeat. When sitting at the bedside of a dying person you love, it is easy to believe that the two of you are the only people in the world and life has stopped, perhaps never to have sunshine again. My days were at Great Party! My evenings were spent sitting at Gran's bedside, sometimes with Mom, and sometimes alone. Mom dealt with the doctors, nurses, and a social worker during the day, but I didn't need them to tell me what I saw. Gran's life force was flagging. Sometimes she would say a few words, but more and more often she said nothing at all, preferring only to have me hold her hand. Around midnight I would slip out, go home to sleep, and begin again early the next day.

Mom said Logan had been by a few times in the morning before school, and at a few odd times when he should have been in school. Without me asking she also said Logan was still spending most nights away from home. He had a new bruise by his left eye to show why. I saw Logan at work several times, but we did not make eye contact, and I didn't talk to him.

On the Friday after Mother's Day I woke up tired and worn. I made a point to pick up my gym bag for my date later in the day with Eric for racquetball. The day went on with the usual business and interruptions. I was so busy that I didn't give a thought to Mom or Gran. I worked in the pensive and sad shadows all of it was creating, but I was on automatic, doing my work to make a living amid heartbreak. It's what one does.

Right after I waved goodbye to Tim and Chef Don, I headed to my car so I could meet Eric for racquetball. As I started my Audi a sensation of falling over a cliff made my head move forward and I knew with certainty, that I needed to head to Forest Grove, not go play racquetball. I called Eric on my way and then tried to focus on driving. But my mind felt overwhelmed, overtaken by images of when I was a teenager. That drive to the hospice was a time in my life where I think God, angels, and all of life were reminding me, telling me something I couldn't quite hear, and I was being guided in that car to where I needed to be.

When I arrived at Gran's room, Mom and Logan were silently watching her sleep. I got another chair and joined them. After half an hour Mom spoke. "Now that you're here, Jacob, I'm going to go home. They called before I could shower this morning, and I rushed right over. I would have called, but when I got here they said she was stabilizing for now. I haven't eaten, and I need to lie down."

I kissed her good-bye and took her seat at the head of the bed. The shades were drawn and it was slowly darkening outside. I looked at Logan, so like I had been at that age: alone, near friendless, feeling like my home life was destroyed. Unloved in the way I needed. That everyone needs.

"Come over here, Logan," I motioned for him to bring his chair by the foot of the bed to sit by me. How could I tell the story in a way that would not just be a story of my life, but a story that could show Logan that he was good, and that a large and happy life lay ahead of him if he would just walk that way.

"Logan, I want to tell you a story about when I was your age. It is also about Gran, but more than either one of us, it is a story that I hope will become yours to use like it helped me. I want you to know a little more about growing up in the turbulent, difficult years you are in right now."

He looked at me, but didn't say anything. I began to talk.

You remember the story I told a few weeks ago about being called to help Gran get ready for Christmas when Pap was in the hospital? Being in the same house with Gran and my sick great-grandmother, Pauline, was the last thing I wanted to do. There I was, half hung over with an insolent attitude that no longer respected any adult. I sat in my black leather jacket and butt-tight jeans with a fifty-dollar haircut I put on my mom's charge card. I was a piece of work, as they say, sure that all I needed to do was give off attitude from my walk to gain respect and put distance between being a child and being a man.

Maybe it was the light of the room from one small bedside lamp, or Pap's silent, slack face resting as though he were a baby in sweet dreams. Maybe it was Gran's voice, so clear and pleading like a child's for one more story before bedtime. "Please God," she said, "he is my life." Whatever it was, I stood at that door, held by the scene, and something in me quivered and fell in pieces I didn't understand. I've heard others say their heart opened up, but I didn't recognize it like that. No, I was too lost to feel that fully. It was only a sliver that gave way, confusing my certainty, and making me feel and see the next two days in a different way.

The next morning Gran kept me busy cleaning, bringing out candles and helping her prepare for Christmas Day. In the afternoon an ambulance brought Pap home. The doctor had sent him home to die. There wasn't anything more they could do for him and it was agreed he would be more comfortable at home. After the ambulance left, Grandma Pauline, Gran, and I stood around him. He opened his eyes and smiled, and Gran leaned and kissed him before sitting down to wait until he again fell asleep.

It was a quiet dinner table that night. The light was low in the dining room and the thrown together, sad little tree in the living room with its uneven lights and misplaced ornaments, did not give us cheer or comfort. The spaghetti a neighbor brought seemed oddly tasteless. The three of us listened for movement from upstairs, but there was none.

"Besides the heart attack, the doctors told me he has pneumonia, and they broke two of his ribs giving him chest compressions. Then there's the diabetes and his heart problems . . ." Gran's voice trailed off and she stared ahead in a disbelief that was protecting her from realizing how great her loss would be. Five minutes passed in silence. "I want you to watch over Matt carefully while I'm gone tomorrow morning to have my hair done and buy some groceries for Christmas Eve."

Another duty, I thought. Couldn't I just go home?

Chapter 13

"We all need help from time to time."
Matthew Arnold

Dreamless and peacefully lost in the sleep of the young, it was a disorienting realization when Pap shook me awake the next morning. "Get up, Jake, get up! We've got things to do."

I sat up, half on my own and half from Pap pulling me up. "What? You're dying. Go sit down." I pointed at a chair in the room.

"Come on, come on. I haven't got anything for your grandmother."

"All right! Leave me alone." Disoriented and indignant at the rude awakening, I pulled my arm away. He stood before me like a pale, frail ghost wearing his old brown boots, a red plaid shirt, and his usual baggy jeans. They were held up with his decades old leather belt hand-carved with pine trees, and a silver buckle studded with a black and white agate in the center—his way of being ready for the day.

"I've made coffee. Get out of that bed." He turned and left.

Grandma Pauline and I emerged from our rooms at the same time and began walking to the kitchen. Both of us had questions in our eyes. We knew Gran had left for her hair appointment, and we were on our own. Pap was agitated as he opened and closed cupboards when we walked in the kitchen. "We've got lots to do today, Jake, and you're not dressed yet. Go get dressed and then you can have some coffee before we leave. Go on."

"Matt, sit down. What's going on? You're sick," Grandma Pauline said.

"I have some Christmas shopping to do, Pauline, and it has to be now."

Whatever was going to happen, I knew I'd better hurry, so I was back downstairs in five minutes, ready to go.

"Here, you drink this on the way," he gave me a mug and indicated I should follow. "We're going for breakfast. There's nothing in this house." I thought he was turning to leave through the front door to get in the truck, but he headed for the Christmas tree instead. "That's the ugliest damn tree I've ever seen." He leaned to unplug the lights and then gripped it by the trunk. Wheezing like a wind tunnel, he lumbered out with the tree to the back patio and dumped it, breaking ornaments, lights and crushing whatever small dignity the tree may have had. "Bet your grandma paid dear for this." He sounded more amused than angry.

"Here, you'll have to shift so sit over here. My ribs are killing me." Pap was in the driver's seat starting the truck in the cold morning. He looked back and forth from the road to me while he worked the pedals and steering wheel, all the while telling me when to do it. "Well, well, looks like those lessons I gave you are paying off. You've learned well."

When we walked in Seabird Café two, maybe three people waved from different parts of the café and a few more nodded. That's what Bothell, Washington was like in those days, though nobody knew Pap had spent the night sleeping like a dead man. People knew each other, but not everything. That morning I started to realize more about that town and the people in it. Tits McGee walked over to Pap as soon as she saw him. As she reached him, she gave me a questioning, slightly angry look as though I'd forced a sick man out of his bed.

"Here, Matt, let me help you to the table. You're a favorite customer."

"And you're my favorite waitress, Nona," he took her arm to steady himself.

As she helped him sit she said, "Matt, it's Christmas and I remember how you and Alwida helped me two years ago. I mean it. Thank you for giving the kids those wooden toys you made and the shirts. It was our Christmas."

"We all need help from time to time. It's what people do."

"No, not all of them. But you and Alwida do." She looked at me." You take care of your grandpa, now. What's for breakfast?"

"Biscuits, gravy, and eggs. For the boy, too. There's nothing better."

Pap was in charge of that day from the moment he woke me, so when he headed home after breakfast, I didn't ask why. I thought he was going to head into the house, but instead he led me to the barn and told me to stand where he pointed. He got on the ladder and reached to the rafters and began throwing down boxes of lights and ornaments to replace the ornaments that now were shattered on the patio.

We were in the middle of carrying them into the house when Gran returned. She saw us carrying boxes as she pulled in the driveway. We continued into the house, but she caught up with us in the backyard, a trembling, angry woman with precise curls around her face. "What are you doing? Are you trying to kill him?"

She waved her arms, heading toward Matt as though she was going to pick him up like an avenging angel. "Jacob, I told you to watch him. I needed you to be the strong one." Then she saw the tree and stopped. "What's going on?" Her voice was louder, near panic.

"Now, Willie, settle down. We're just getting ready for Christmas. That was a pathetic tree, and you know it."

I could see Grandma Pauline at the kitchen door watching what was going on. Neither one of us had ever seen Pap and Gran like this. "Matt! Get in the house now. You need to rest. How could you do this, Jake?"

I lifted an arm to protest, but I saw Grandma Pauline put her finger to her lips to quiet me. "This isn't right, this just isn't right. What do you think you are doing?" The fear and near hysteria in Gran's voice surprised me.

"Willie, *Willie*, come here, it's all right. See? I'm all right. Everything's all right. Come here," he held his arms open. She walked to him and buried her face in his chest. Sobs worked their way out of her in halting, choking sounds.

Pap held her close until her sobbing subsided. Suddenly she pulled herself away and started towards the kitchen door. "Come inside, Matt." Her voice was deep and now in control.

He did look like he appreciated sitting in his usual chair in the living room, but I could also tell he was doing this only to make Gran settle down. Without her there, he intended to plow through his plans for the day, whatever they were.

Gran sat in her chair on the other side of a table with a lamp on it. They both faced the television, but she abruptly turned to him. Like mute puppets, Grandma Pauline and I sat on the couch watching. For a minute everyone was quiet, seeming to catch their breath, and settle our minds on a situation none of us understood.

"Matt, you've got to rest. Don't think you can start cleaning the barn. You're not going to get better if you don't rest, and I'm not putting those lights back on that damn tree."

"I know that, Willie. Now you just go about your day. I'll be fine. Jake and I will stay in the rest of the day."

"Jake, it's your job to keep an eye on him and not let him go running around town. Do you understand?"

"Yes."

"Mother, you have to be in charge, too. They aren't being responsible."

"All right."

She took in a big breath and slowly released it. "All right, then. Everyone understands. Now tomorrow is Christmas Eve and I still have lots to do. I need to get a few things, so I'm going to go to the store. I need a few groceries."

We all sat quietly, eager for her to leave, all of us for different reasons. She got up slowly, went to the master bathroom, freshened her face, calmed herself down, got a new book of checks, and returned to Matt. She kissed his cheek and said, "Rest, Matt," before at last leaving. No one got up, or said a word while she started the car, backed out of the driveway and headed to town, though all three of us visibly relaxed our bodies against the chair and couch.

I leaned back, watched Pap close his eyes, and wondered how long I should politely wait before suggesting he go up to bed, so I could call Mom and ask her when she was coming for me. I knew there was a party that night at a kid's house whose parents were going to be late at another party, and I could almost taste the bourbon I'd come to enjoy. My mouth watered. Beside me, I smelled the roses Pap always had sent in the vase on the table beside me. It was the smell of my grandparents' house.

Pap's eyes were closed, his breathing steady and resting. After fifteen minutes, he opened his eyes as though all he'd done was blink and said, "Are you finished sleeping over there, Jake?"

"Huh?"

"We've got shopping to do, too."

"But, Pap . . ."

"No, buts, let's go boy." He was getting up.

"Matt, you need to stay," Pauline said.

"Pauline, I need to buy Alwida's Christmas present."

In minutes Pap and I were in the truck with him guiding and me shifting, on our way to Alderwood Mall in Lynnwood, Washington.

A dozen busy shoppers passed us as we slowly made our way to the mall doors. He mostly walked on his own, but I walked closely because every third step or so he would put his large workman's hand on my shoulder to balance himself.

"We're going to Sears," Pap announced.

It's difficult to tell the story of this day without sounding like I'm exaggerating about how I felt inside. My sense of awareness slowly opened through the morning, expanding as we walked through the middle of the rush of shoppers who jostled us with their shopping bags.

On a clock, I noticed the time was twelve thirty, but it seemed as though Pap and I were walking in a time tunnel of today, this hour, this moment. He lead us to the jewelry counter and heavily laid down his forearm on the glass for support. I knew his sense of strength and power he had always commanded was being deeply challenged when he stood taller, forcing himself to endure the pain of broken ribs.

A tall woman with lots of makeup on and inch long red nails was adjusting the display of pearl necklaces. "Miss, miss . . ." Pap said.

She blankly looked at us.

"Miss, I need a really great gift for my wife."

"Yes," her face wasn't any more interested.

"Something just right for her."

"Yes," she flourished her hand, indicating the display in the case as though she assumed it held something the wife of a sick man who didn't look like his bank account had much, would love. As we looked down, two women came up next to Pap and began oohing and aahing over a brooch.

"I'd like to see that," one of them said, pointing.

"Certainly," the sales lady said, devoting herself to them.

We looked another minute, but then Pap indicated we should go. When we turned around to leave the woman didn't glance at us.

"Where now, Pap?"

"I'll show you." Again, it was a slow walk through crowds, but we made it to another department store's jewelry counter. This time we were at the emerald display. We commented on several pieces before a sales clerk holding a sack with a bow passed us on her way to a man standing a few feet away. After she gave him the sack she came our way again. I think Pap was realizing the rush of this shopping day, and he raised his arm to slow her.

"Miss, I need a gift for my wife," she slowed and looked at him. His voice softened, "Let me tell you about my wife . . ."

"Do you see anything you like?" she interrupted. I've always remembered the challenge in her words, forced through pursed lips.

I looked at my Pap again. His voice had a caressing ring of love I'd only heard between Pap and Gran. I felt all through me that I was witnessing a seldom expressed pureness, an understanding that everything could be gone tomorrow. His voice and words held story, love, giving, and caring through hardships. The saleswoman was being invited, but she could not hear or see. Her lips tightened, and her shoulders moved in agitation. Like the last salesclerk, she did a flourish over the counter, "This is all we have left. Do you see anything you like?"

"No, not yet," Now his voice had a tinge of worry, a tone I'd never heard.

"Louise, can you come over here?" A woman who had authority in her voice had called the sales lady away, but before she left she leaned and whispered, "There isn't much time today."

Pap turned away, still leaning on the counter.

"Let's go, boy. There's nothing here."

As we drove out of the mall parking lot, I didn't have any idea where we were going and I wasn't sure how much longer he could be away from bed.

"We're going to Jerry's."

Walking into Jerry Padgett's Pharmacy on the town's old Main Street was like walking into the house of a friend after being in a crowded bus station. The rectangular pharmacy with it's long lunch counter was warm and quiet: a fragment left from history.

Three men sitting at the counter turned and waved. "Hey, Matt, see you've got the boy today" one off them said. The waitress pouring coffee waved. Two children looked at a toy display while their mother browsed picked-over Christmas wrapping.

"Matt! We have your diabetes medication," Margie, a large, smiling woman, appeared from out of the short aisles on the right side. "You look like you could enjoy sitting down. Here, give this man an orange juice," she hailed a woman behind the counter as she led Matt to the last stool.

"Thanks, Margie."

"I've been expecting you. I know you didn't ask for it, but you've been by every year for it. We have *White Shoulders* for you."

"Thanks, Margie, there are lots of reasons to love you."

"Remind old man Jerry about that, will you?" She laughed and headed back for the medication and the cologne. While we waited, I again thought of a drink and the party that night, but the party's allure was fading. The magic gift of this day was starting to sink into me.

"Well, boy, we're getting our shopping done."

I was sure as soon as we got home he would want to sleep. Instead, he headed to the liquor cabinet in the dining room. "Would you like a Manhattan?"

I just looked at him. He knows, I thought. He knows I drink too much.

"You're old enough," he said. He turned and mixed each of us a Manhattan.

"Are you still alive?" Pauline's large farm voice rang from her bedroom.

"Yes, Pauline, I'm alive and kicking."

Drinks in hand, Pap headed to his easy chair, and I sat in Gran's. I felt peace. It settled on me like an invisible blanket, and I didn't know where it came from, but the quiet of this house, being aware that Grandma Pauline was upstairs, the presence of this man who had always been of few words, the expectation of my grandmother's return, knowing my mother would also come, all of this tumbled together in a yet to be understood realization.

"It's nice to have you here, Jake." Pap's voice was soft, and it felt like he was the one who settled the blanket of peace around me. We heard Gran pull in the driveway. She came in, dropped sacks by the door, then appeared in the living room. I didn't know about Pap, but my body felt the oozing comfort of the drink, and I smiled when I saw Gran.

"What have you two been doing?" I followed her gaze, which was fixed on Pap. He did look grayish-green and very tired.

Pap lifted his elbow to the arm of the chair and opened his large hand toward her. "Willie, it's okay."

She slipped her hand in his and looked into his eyes. The she backed away and came toward where I was sitting in her chair. I got out and went to the couch.

Grandma Pauline slowly came down the stairs and walked to the other end of the couch. "What are you doing up, Mom?" Gran asked.

"Your daughter Mary needs my help."

"Oh?"

"She's on her way to pick me up to go make bows for the Christmas tree."

Grandma Pauline was queen of making bows. Gran had given up all effort to learn how to tie a bow properly, Mom was a fair student of bow-making, I was considered an apprentice, and Pap had refused all invitations to learn, saying he was master of wrapping gifts and that was enough talent.

"Then we need another tree." Gran's voice was stronger, fixed to a goal. She stood up. "If you're making bows, we need to go get a tree. I'm making coffee and hot choc-olate." She headed to the kitchen. Her sudden boost in energy seemed to recharge Pap, too, because his color be-gan to change to a clearer, rosier shade.

There were two short knocks and Mom appeared at the front door. "Ready, Grandma?"

"I sure am. We have lots of work to do."

"How's it going, Jake?"

The near empty Manhattan was on the table next to me and I hoped she hadn't noticed. "Okay."

By the time Grandma Pauline was bundled in her coat and hat, Gran was back with two thermoses and cups. Mom's big sedan headed one way, and the three of us headed the other way in the truck that would carry the real Christmas tree. Everyone was ready to do their part.

I stopped talking and looked over at Logan, wonder-ing if I had gone on too long.

"Where did you get the tree, Mr. Buchanan?"

"Are you sure you want to hear all this?"

His head bobbed up and down. "Yes."

I looked over at Gran. She was in the peaceful, deep sleep of children.

All three of us were jammed into the front seat of the truck. I held the thermoses by the passenger window, and Gran sat in the middle, shifting when Pap nodded his head. It didn't occur to me to ask where we were going. I think I knew. This day was falling into a story that didn't have room for what wasn't real. We were headed toward a Christmas tree farm in Carnation, Washington. A few flakes started to fall from the darkened sky, but they were not enough to do any more than evaporate when they hit the windshield.

A half dozen cars and trucks were in the parking lot when we pulled in to Lawrence Heard's tree farm. Larry was helping a family tie a tree to the top of their car. He waved and yelled, "Alwida, Matt, how are you doing?"

Gran was distracted, still getting out of the truck and arranging the thermoses. I was standing next to Pap on the driver's side and saw him lean heavily on the door before he sighed.

"Come on, we gotta pick a tree," I said to him.

"No, you're old enough, Jake. You are in charge of picking the tree."

Larry began walking toward us. He was a tall, thin man with high ruddy cheeks from being outside so much. He stopped when he got a close look at Pap.

"We're here for our tree," said Gran as she came around. "This is our grandson, Jake."

"Nice to meet you, Jake."

"Nice to meet you," I said.

Pap handed Larry a rope. I was already holding my chain saw. Pap and Gran led the way to the trees while Larry and I fell back a dozen paces.

"I've known your grandparents since they moved here from Reno."

I nodded.

"Matt came in the bank where I worked to open an account."

"Oh."

"From the first day he seemed like a friend. More than a customer."

We walked a few paces, then Pap turned around. "Tell us when you see the right tree, Jake."

"I met your grandmother a few weeks later when they invited me over for dinner," Larry said.

"Oh." I wasn't really listening. I needed to keep my eyes out for a tree.

"She's a good cook, Alwida."

"Yes, she is."

"Well, we became better friends. I've always been a loner sort. My parents both died within a year of each other when I was nineteen and I was their only kid. There wasn't much of a family."

"That's too bad."

"So I never did get much practice at being around people."

I finally looked at him. He seemed to be talking a lot for a loner.

"Jake, how about this tree?" Gran pointed and yelled from about twenty feet up the trail.

"Alwida, let him choose," Matt kept walking. Snow was dusting our shoulders and beginning to dress the trees.

"Here's what I want to tell you, Jake," Larry finally said. "Your grandpa could see I didn't fit in with the banking culture. Not my sort of life to be in a suit, sitting at a desk. He'd spend time talking to me when he came in. Encouraged me to get into something else."

Larry stopped talking and I thought he was finished. I walked to a tree a few feet from the trail and went around it. The backside wasn't perfect.

"Then I met a woman," he picked up again when I returned to his side. "She meant a lot to me, so I stayed at the bank to show her we could live well, but when I asked her too marry me, she said no."

"Oh."

"It was terrible. The bleakest time of my life. One night it just all hit me. Hit me bad. My parents were dead, I didn't fit at the bank and everyone knew it. The woman I loved didn't love me."

I glanced at him, and for the first time I saw his nervousness as he talked. I stopped when I spied another tree behind him.

"I was near taking my life. I had a gun. It felt like, well, awful and still so easy to do."

I was headed to the tree, but looked over at Larry and stopped when I saw the pain in his eyes. Gran and Pap had turned around to see why we had stopped and began walking back.

"But your grandpa just happened to call while I was thinking mighty strongly about it and invited me over for dinner. He'd been in that day and he could tell I was down. His and Alwida's caring saved my life."

"Did you see a tree?" Gran was almost upon us, with Pap trailing.

"Uh, yeah, over here." I led everyone over to inspect the seven foot Douglas fir. Snow weight separated the branches, displaying its symmetry. After I'd walked around it twice and saw that Gran looked pleased with it, I proclaimed it the one and everyone backed away while I started the chain saw.

Larry and I carried the tree between us and Gran held the chain saw. When we got back to the parking lot Larry indicated where Gran could take Pap to sit while we tied the tree to the truck. After it was secure, he walked over to me and put his hand on my shoulder to gain my attention.

"What you need to know, Jake, is how special your grandpa is and how lucky you are to have someone like him in your life. Alwida, too."

At that age it embarrassed me to acknowledge the importance of old people, so I shrugged my shoulders, but when I turned away to check if the tree was secured, I saw Gran and Pap sitting on a covered porch and I remembered how they had looked the first time I saw them at the airport when I was nine and Mom was beaten up and wearing sunglasses. I felt it deeply at that moment. That man and woman were my home every bit as my Mom was. They were what was making me and they deserved something good.

"Yes, Mr. Heard. They are special."

There weren't any more customers in the parking lot. Whoever still needed a Christmas tree would be waiting until tomorrow on Christmas Eve. The late afternoon snow had made it difficult to get to the tree farm, so as we drove away, the truck made the only tracks in the road.

"Wave at Lawrence, Jake. Matt can't," Gran told me. I opened the window, stuck my head out, and gave one wide, slow wave.

A nurse had come into the room and began checking Gran to make sure she was sleeping peacefully.

"Wow, Mr. Buchanan, that's some story." Logan's voice had a tone of admiration I immediately wanted to turn into something else: a tool.

"Logan, the power of the story isn't just about Gran and Pap." He looked interested in my answer as I continued. "It's about what they did. It's about what everyone can do with their life story."

"What do you mean?"

The nurse had finished checking Gran, and though she appeared interested in what I was saying, she left the room and I heard her walk down the hall.

"In their small way, in their quiet lives that are easily overlooked, they were warriors."

"Warriors?"

"Yes, they always thought to do the small, good thing for other people. They were quietly ferocious in changing the lives of many people."

"How did they change yours?"

The snow started coming down harder, so hard in fact, that as familiar as Pap was with the country roads that led us home, he drove very slowly to pay attention. I remember that ride so well. Uninterrupted Christmas music was playing on the truck radio, a caring man was driving us home, a loving woman poured me hot chocolate she had made just for me from a thermos, and a tree I had chosen and cut was tied to the back of the truck. The snow was enclosing my world, enclosing my thoughts in a way that helped me see deeper into myself and the people who meant the most to me, the very people I had been fighting against with my teenage drinking, partying, and attitude.

I felt a peace and an understanding wash through me in a way I had never felt before. I was loved and I did love. That late afternoon drive was one of the happiest, if not the happiest, time of my life. Pap took a wrong turn, and we drove a good half mile before we recognized the dairy farm down a road we shouldn't have turned on, but at least we knew where we were, and now Pap could lead us back.

After Pap helped me carry in the tree, he headed to his chair in the living room. "I'll watch." He was breathing hard, but seemed content. When Gran returned to the kitchen, Pap motioned me over to whisper in my ear. "Jake, it's your responsibility to get the White Shoulders out of the sack on the floor at the back of the guest closet and hide it in the tree when it's decorated."

I smiled, pleased to be a part of my grandparents' love story. Almost as soon as I got the tree positioned to Gran's standard in front of the living room window, Mom and Grandma Pauline drove up.

"That mother of yours is a slave driver, Jake!" Grandma Pauline declared.

"And that would be unlike you, Mother?" asked Gran of her own farm working mother.

"At least she comes by it honestly then. Jake, go help the slave driver bring the thousand bows in."

Every silver bow was perfect.

Chapter 14

"Do you know the worth of your own soul?"
Matthew Arnold

"That was a nice Christmas story, Mr. Buchanan."

"Yes, that night was the first time I really understood why Christmas, especially Christmas Eve, has always been so important to my family. It brings us together and is our way of renewing to one another the importance of home and each other."

"Yeah, that must be nice."

"I have always known I could go home. In those years I might have gotten in trouble for something I'd just done, but I knew I was always welcome home."

Logan was nodding his head, but he was silent. I knew I was stepping very closely to the pain he was living with in his own home.

"It's late, Logan, I'll drive you home." We got up, I kissed Gran good night and we headed out. The fresh spring air seemed out of place, a very strange wake-up call, after a Christmas story. As we walked to the car

I tried to think of what to say next, what would be of use for this boy. We were out of the parking lot and had driven a few blocks before I said anything.

"It took me years before I really realized how so many people I met that day gave me a piece to the puzzle of who my grandparents were and how their kindness and love that they gave to so many was for me, too."

Logan was staring ahead, so I continued after saying a silent prayer to myself that whatever I said would help this boy. "I was still a kid, too, Logan, and I partied, but that day was the beginning of real growing up.

"Even the two busy salesclerks who didn't have time for Pap showed me how much he loved Gran and how much married people can love each other. It was her Christmas he was worried about, not his."

"He sure knew a lot of people in the town."

"Yes."

"My grandma was like that, too. She would always take food to the neighbors, and she spent hours knitting things for babies. When I was over there, she would always make such a fuss over me."

"Sometimes, Logan, memory is all we have, but we can use it to help us through."

The house was dark when we drove up to it. "Well, thanks for the ride home, Mr. Buchanan."

The next days were a blur. I moved constantly, always trying to finish some task. At the office there were clients and potential clients to call, bids to prepare, vendors to work with, a staff to keep running well, and the ever closer, hovering event for Cameron Enterprises. At home Mom needed help with kitchen work and laundry. Both of us were caught in a bubble of time where everything we did was to find things to make it pass, or sometimes keeping it from passing. We traded off sitting with Gran and often sat silently together with her in the evenings. Each day she faded a shade further from us. Her eyes opened less often. She held our hands with less pressure. The nurses treated her more tenderly.

"I've been thinking about your father lately, Jake," Mom said one night as we sat together.

"Oh?"

"Yes. We both need to settle our feelings more about him. It's never good to hurt people like he has, but he has been important to both of us."

"I don't hate him, Mom. I just don't understand him."

"And maybe you never will, and that's okay. Try and remember the goodness he also has."

I saw Logan a time or two as he worked at Great Party!, and a nurse told me about the occasional visits of a teenage boy. It was after eight o'clock Friday night when I was able to get to Gran's side. Mom was sitting on the far side of the bed by the window, so I got another chair and sat on the side by the door. I curiously motioned to a glass vase with a single red rose amid baby's breath.

"Sadie said Logan brought it by this morning before I got here."

We stayed until after eleven and Mom returned before eight the next morning. We traded off and on though the day, relieving each other only for breaks to stretch our legs and get coffee. Food, work, and the rest of the world did not exist in this ever more dense bubble of watching Gran slip toward death.

That night Mom left after eight, and I leaned back, closed my eyes and asked God to make it easy for my Gran. Memories floated through me of two days before Pap died. He spent most of his time in his chair wrapped in blankets. Friends visited. Gran quietly talked to him and held his hand. Mom read the newspaper to him and tucked in his blankets. One evening Gran and Mom were at the grocery store, and I was assigned to sit by him. It seemed an effort for him to talk, so I was quiet. Suddenly, he turned to me when I thought he was falling asleep and said, "Jacob, do you know the worth of your own soul?"

I stared at him.

"You have one. Take care of it. Treasure it. Value it." Then he closed his eyes and was silent until Gran and Mom got back.

I felt like I was beginning to understand. Exhausted, I left Gran after midnight to a fitful, dream-filled half-sleep.

Sunday morning Mom and I were in the kitchen taking small bites of toast and sips of coffee before heading to see Gran. I stood up without knowing why and walked to the living room where clear spring morning light was flooding in on the oil painting of Gran's thirty-year-old face. She looked so dear and alive. I returned to the kitchen. Seconds after sitting at the table, I felt a sweeping roll of familiar energy brushing against my back and then surrounding all of me before sweeping away.

"Mom, I just felt something."

"What, Jake?"

"I think I just felt Gran pass. I think she just died and is saying goodbye to us."

Mom turned to look at me. Slowly, she set down her coffee cup. "Let's go."

We headed out the back door toward the car when we heard the telephone ringing in the now locked house. We knew what the message was so we continued toward the car.

"She was lurching out of the bed, reaching toward something," Sadie told us an hour later. Mom and I looked at each other, both of us sure Gran had seen Matt.

Time now had a peculiar air of standing on a mountain peak. I had trouble breathing in that thin air, my heart heavy as it worked to survive, but my sight was far, the panorama before me was an open view of more than I had ever seen at one time. The confusion of the last months disappeared.

I was keenly aware of it when I called Liz to tell her. Ann promised to send Liz, and with a voice softened with care that I hadn't heard for years, she said, "Thanks for finding the box, Jake."

"Ann, tell me. What is in that box that has made it so important to you?"

She was quiet for a few seconds, but I had time, more time than I knew what to do with that day, so I waited. "Three things. First, the Christmas ornaments you bought the year Liz was born. Then a photo of my parents' wedding. I thought I had another, but I don't so I needed to find that one. Then, well, then . . ." she stalled but I was quiet, ". . . photos of our wedding. I thought I didn't want them, but I do."

"Why?"

"Jake, you'll think this is silly, but here goes. I think it's important to have them for Liz. She needs to see what ended so terribly for us had a happy start. That she brought joy to us and it was us, not her, that messed things up."

Well, I thought, the snake's skin is a sign of transformation after all. Maybe what we think we know about people is only a fraction.

I went in to the office at mid-afternoon on Monday. Mom was making arrangements for the funeral, and I needed to keep myself busy as much as check on things. Everyone said kind words or gave me sympathetic looks, but business always continues. They scurried about me doing what needed to be done.

"Where's Logan?" It struck me that I had only heard of his visits to Gran, but I hadn't seen him since I'd told him the story. Chef Don was in the midst of people moving around, gathering items for the Cameron Enterprises event. Why had Cameron felt so overwhelming and big? Now it was a small thing, a blip that needed attention, but would never be as important as the human beings who worked for me, who were scurrying around me now. Nor would a faceless company that represented numbers on my budget and events calendar ever mean as much as my family.

"He's supposed to be here." Chef Don was looking at Melissa and Todd who stood five feet away.

Todd glanced at me, but then focused on Don. "He called last night and said he wouldn't be back. Saturday night he and his mom started back to Texas. Just the two of them. His mom has a sister there."

The rose was his goodbye gesture, I thought.

Mom went to bed at eight o'clock that night. The next day people would begin flying or driving in so she wanted to rest as much as possible. Shadow and I were left alone for the first time in weeks. He placed his long snout on my knee and looked mournfully into my eyes. Yes, he knew all the changes that were taking place around him.

I looked at the driftwood that Gran had polished and which now sat on my desk. The value and work of her life remained. Did I see it? In this thin air on a lonely mental mountaintop all by myself, did I see what was really going on? Outside of the grief that had not yet settled in, did I see the panorama of life that my grandmother, Alwida Emerson Stewart Arnold, had lived?

Without her around, would I remember the power of her love and acceptance, the fiery strength of her spirit that always continued in spite of hardship? Would I always remember to make a home like she and Pap had where family could return for replenishment and love? Could I reach out like they had to neighbors, friends, even strangers they met and give comfort in what appeared to be small ways, but was not small at all? For many people they made a difference.

Could my story of being a confused and angry teenager who was changed by my grandparents have helped, in the smallest way, to lead Logan through his troubles? The last time I saw Logan was when I'd taken him home from the hospital. I remember looking at his back as he walked away and thinking, It doesn't happen overnight, Logan. I didn't stop drinking or suddenly change after those three days in December. Instead, that time with Pap and Gran had been like a seed that grew within until it lead me to adulthood. It was likely I would never know what happened to Logan, but I had not reached out expecting guaranteed results. I had told him the story to give him hope to find his way.

That night's sleep was strangely peaceful. When I woke the next morning I felt a peace in the very middle of my heart that felt as though it were glowing from a love I didn't comprehend. When I turned my head to see the clock, the feeling started to fade as a dream, but its peace remained with me for many days. Gran, I believed, was in this peace.

Airports have dramatically changed from the 1980s to now. I was no longer able to stand and watch the trail of people leave the plane until I saw Liz as Gran and Pap had when they waited for Mom and me. Now I was in my car in a parking lot with dozens of strangers in their cars, all of us watching the ever changing, flashing sign of a dozen arrivals that gave us permission to drive to the passenger arrival lanes. The routines of the world had changed just enough since that day Mom brought me home to Gran and Pap that it would be easy to say the two reunions at the airport were completely different. But I was learning my history lesson. They were not so different.

I was welcoming home my daughter who was working in a child's way to balance the changes of her life. The frailties of her parents had disrupted her life, and it was up to Ann in her way, and me in mine, to forgive one another as we could, and regain the balance and strength of our lives so we could pass that on to our daughter.

About the Author

Slade Austin has spent the majority of his career in marketing and public relations. He never intended to write a novel, but *Three Days in December* is a story from his heart, taken from parts of his life that have been meaningful and compelling.

One of the most important issues he wanted to address in the book is the abuse of women and children, whether emotional or physical. *Three Days* encompasses many of the hard realities of life, but Austin believes that through these hard realities, one can find hope and eventually peace.

Austin grew up in Steubenville, Ohio and now resides in Salt Lake City, Utah.